FROM MONGOLIA'S DESOLATION ROAD
TO A HIDDEN PREHISTORIC VALLEY, AN AMAZING
DISCOVERY HATCHES INTO AN ADVENTURE OF
DANGER, MYSTERY AND DEATH....

INDIANA JONES—The renowned archaeologist and adventurer has come face-to-face with the greatest wonders of the world. But nothing could prepare him for the stunning secret that awaited him in the heart of far Mongolia.

SISTER JOAN STARBUCK—The American missionary believes in the goodness of humankind. And in a long, harrowing journey full of violence and treachery, she may find it yet.

LAO CHE—This ruthless Chinese gangster made his fortune in opium and white slavery. Now he's sent one of his best and most lethal assassins after the only man who dares to cross him: Indiana Jones.

GENERAL TZI—The reigning warlord of Mongolia, he tracks his prey with a ferocious pack of wild dogs. His respect for Indiana Jones is so great that the barbarian chieftain has vowed to track down and kill the famed adventurer—and to eat the heart of his erstwhile foe.

TZEN KHAN—A descendant of the infamous Genghis Khan, this renegade Mongol bandit joins Indy in his flight from General Tzi. But is he as noble as he seems—or is he only waiting for the right moment to betray his newfound ally?

GRANGER—The big-game hunter is one of Indy's oldest and closest friends. Before this expedition is over the two will fight side-by-side in a desperate last stand against an army of enemies—and only a miracle can save them.

THE INDIANA JONES SERIES
Ask your bookseller for the books you have missed

INDIANA JONES™

AND THE

DINOSAUR EGGS

MAX McCOY

BANTAM BOOKS
NEW YORK   TORONTO   LONDON   SYDNEY   AUCKLAND

INDIANA JONES AND THE DINOSAUR EGGS
A Bantam Book

PUBLISHING HISTORY
Bantam mass market edition published March 1996
Bantam reissue / April 2008

Published by
Bantam Dell
A Division of Random House, Inc.
New York, New York

Bantam Books and the rooster colophon are registered trademarks of Random House, Inc.

ISBN 978-0-553-56193-7

Printed in the United States of America
Published simultaneously in Canada

www.bantamdell.com

OPM   14 13 12 11 10 9 8 7 6 5

For W. C. Jameson:
treasure hunter, songwriter,
scholar, and friend

Mongolia, a land of mystery, of paradox and promise!... The badlands were almost paved with white fossil bones and all represented animals unknown to us. Granger picked up a few bits of fossil eggshell which he thought were from long-extinct birds. No one suspected, then, that these were the first dinosaur eggs to be discovered by modern man....
—ROY CHAPMAN ANDREWS

AND THE

DINOSAUR
EGGS

Prologue

CASTLE OF THE DAMNED

Forteresse Malevil
Marseilles, France
October 1933

The meaty fist hit Indiana Jones like a sledgehammer, splitting his upper lip against his front teeth and sending a kaleidoscope of colors dancing behind his eyes. If Indy had ever been hit harder, he could not remember it.

His head lolled back against the chest of the French giant who held his arms pinned to his sides. The world grew dim and Indy was afraid he would black out. Then the coppery taste of blood filled his mouth and anger brought him back.

Indy managed a bloody, lopsided grin.

"Who taught you to punch?" he asked. "Your grandmother?"

His attacker—a twin to the giant who held Indy's arms—did not speak English, but he understood the insulting tone in which the comment was delivered. He hit Indy again, only harder, and this time in the stomach.

"Schoolboy taunts, Dr. Jones? I would have expected something more substantial from a man of your reputation. And I have waited such a long time to meet you."

René Belloq's lilting voice echoed from the walls of the dank cavern. The French archaeologist was sitting on an upright yellow drum, his legs crossed, his trademark white hat pulled low over his eyes. On a cluttered desk behind him, beneath a bare bulb hanging from a frayed wire that descended from the ceiling, was a half-consumed bottle of the local white wine and an abandoned plate of cheese. Stacked around the desk were packing crates of every size and description, stenciled on their sides with ports of call from around the world.

In Belloq's lap was Indy's wallet, and he studied it as he might an artifact that had been plucked from the sands of time. Indy's bullwhip, revolver, and fedora lay at Belloq's feet.

"I had hoped for a more amiable meeting," Belloq said. "I apologize for the rough treatment you have received at the hands of the Daguerre brothers, but I did not know who you were and in my line of work I cannot afford to take chances. I have followed your career with some interest in the *Herald-Tribune,* especially your exploits in Central and South America. I had even dreamed of the day when we might work together, but alas, it is not meant to be."

"Good," Indy spat.

"I'm afraid not, Dr. Jones," Belloq said. "Tell me, what are you doing here? I imagine your Titian-haired girlfriend thought you quite clever as you both followed me from shop to shop along the Canebière and then here, to Forteresse Malevil, this evening. Why have you dogged me so intently, Dr. Jones?"

"Business," Indy wheezed.

Belloq laughed.

"It is most certainly not pleasure," he said. Belloq hummed a few bars of the "Marsellaise" as he picked up Indy's revolver and shook out the cartridges into the palm of his hand. He put the shells in the breast pocket of his white jacket, along with Indy's wallet, then closed the revolver.

"This is my neighborhood, Dr. Jones, and all of Provence is my domain. A hundred pairs of eyes followed your amateurish attempt at surveillance—ah, what a marvelous French word!—and a hundred lips reported your movements back to me. What were you hoping to steal from me?"

Belloq spoke to the thugs in French, and they stepped away. Indy slumped to his knees, but managed to catch himself before he fell onto the flagstones.

Belloq offered the Webley.

Indy cautiously took the revolver and returned it to its holster. Belloq then picked up the bullwhip and began inspecting it, just as he had done with Indy's wallet.

"Curious that you would carry such an arcane weapon," Belloq said. "But it is somehow fitting, considering the American affinity for artless and brutal things."

"It's not a weapon," Indy said. "It's a *tool*. It comes in handy."

"I imagine it does, Dr. Jones. Just as I find the Daguerre twins occasionally handy. This business of yours," Belloq urged. "Tell me more."

"It's a long story."

"Time is short," Belloq said. "You have stumbled into my lair at a crucial moment, the spring tide of the full moon. Speak quickly, because my guests will be arriving shortly."

Indy drew himself up to a sitting position. Through swollen eyes, he examined the canister upon which Belloq sat. It was marked with a skull-and-crossbones warning, and a German legend that identified it as nerve gas of the type that had been used during the world war.

A few yards from where Belloq sat, the flagstones ended. The single bulb hanging over the desk did little to reach into the vast darkness beyond, but Indy could hear the sound of waves lapping against the stones.

"I came here to make a deal," Indy said, and rubbed his jaw. "Reliable sources said that a certain artifact—a fully articulated crystal skull, period unknown—was for sale on the black market here. And the black market in antiquities means you, Belloq. Everybody knows that."

"So it seems," Belloq said, and gave a little salute.

"I'm here for the skull, Belloq. The museum will pay your price, no questions asked."

"You should have held on to the skull when you had it, my friend," Belloq said. "I understand from my Italian contact, a charming *fascista*, that you once had the skull in your possession—briefly."

"Name your price."

"You are hardly in a position to bargain, Dr. Jones. Besides, I doubt if your museum would be willing to pay the equivalent of two million American dollars for it."

"Nobody has that kind of money."

"Some do, I'm afraid. I have a rather important buyer."

"No museum in the world would pay even half that."

"Show some imagination, my friend," Belloq said. "The skull has appeal far beyond that of a mere museum piece."

"You're bluffing."

"There is no advantage for me in bluffing," Belloq said sadly. "No amount of money is worth double-crossing the kind of people I'm dealing with. Alas, that is the disadvantage of the black market— if I ran a legitimate operation, I could steal all I wanted with a briefcase and there would be no need for the likes of business associates such as Claude and Jean Daguerre."

Hearing the mention of their names, the brothers grinned.

"Look," Indy said. "Maybe we could work something out—"

"You are too late." Belloq looked at his watch. "The skull is no longer for sale. The exchange will be completed in minutes. But do not despair, Dr. Jones. Time has a way of undoing the best-laid plans, and in the end we really are only stewards of the things we possess. Things become lost, buried, forgotten, and fall into yet other hands."

"What do you mean?"

"Take this cavern, for instance, and the fortress above it. In medieval times it belonged to my family. My ancestral home. But it was taken from us when we backed the wrong side of the throne—we are Templars, you see, and some say that the soul of Jesus Christ lives in us. Alas, others have taken particular exception to that notion. Forteresse Malevil was occupied by a succession of ignoble squatters, fell into disrepair during the revolution, and now is again the center of a family business, even if that business is underground in more than one sense. In the same fashion, Dr. Jones, perhaps the skull will return to you—or to your descendants."

"I can't wait that long."

"Why do you need it so desperately?" Belloq asked. "You have more than a professional interest in this chunk of articulated quartz, do you not? Surely you are not superstitious enough to believe the curse...or perhaps you have been seduced by the dark promise of the skull."

Belloq looked at his watch again.

"Ah, high tide."

"Name your price," Indy said. "Anything."

"I *am* greedy," Belloq said. "Under other circumstances, I would make you—how do you say it?—pay through your nose. But backing out on the deal I already have would be akin to suicide, and I am much too self-centered for that kind of foolishness."

"Who," Indy asked, "could be bad enough to scare *you*?"

The water beyond the flagstones began to swell.

The illuminated prow of a German U-boat undulated just beneath the surface, followed by the exposed snout of a forty-five-millimeter deck gun. In the glow of the running lights, Indy could see the

telltale bulge of a torpedo tube running alongside
her nose.

"Since Hitler became chancellor earlier this
year," Belloq said, "the Nazis have launched a desperate effort to locate arcane treasures with supposed supernatural powers. The Crystal Skull is
high on their list."

The cavern was filled with the insistent hum of
electric motors and the gastric sounds of ballast
tanks being trimmed as the submarine fought to
maintain its neutral, partially submerged buoyancy
in the confines of the cavern.

The conning tower, bristling with periscope and
radio aerials, rode a half-dozen feet above the water
and its fairwater carried the faint outline of a
double-blocked alphanumeric, *U-357.* Unless one
was standing beside the boat, identification of it
would be impossible.

A pair of sailors emerged from the hatch on top
of the conning tower and clambered down to the
saddlelike ballast tanks awash with seawater. Slung
across their backs were Schmeisser submachine
guns. After making fast lines to the centuries-old
rings set into the flagstones, the sailors took up posi-
tions flanking Belloq.

The Daguerre twins drew their own guns.

"Put them away, you idiots," Belloq snapped in
French.

The captain of the *U-357,* a tired-looking former

career officer named Wagner, had watched from the observation platform of the conning tower as the boat was secured. Now satisfied, he called down the open hatch.

Franz Kroeger squeezed his shoulders through the hatch and emerged on deck. Kroeger was everything that Wagner was not: young, tall, blond, and with a freshly pressed black uniform that emphasized his perfectly proportioned body. The uniform was devoid of insignia, except for a pair of lightning bolts on the collar. Kroeger was a colonel in the newly formed Leibstandarte SS, Hitler's personal guard, and if things went awry, he wanted no evidence that would point directly back to the former paperhanger who had become, just a few months before, chancellor of Germany.

Kroeger's boots rang sharply on the iron rungs as he descended the con. The deck covering the starboard saddle tank of the *U-357* was in thigh-deep water, but Kroeger managed a swagger as he waded across.

Once up on the flagstones, Kroeger paused and drew a cigarette case from his breast pocket. He lit a Players cigarette with an American lighter, and the smoke wreathed his young blond head like a wicked halo.

"Monsieur Belloq," he said; in his thick German accent the name came out "Bellosh." "I apologize, but my English is better than my French, and I'm sure that your German would grate upon my ears. You may call me Franz, and I am at your service." His heels snapped together sharply and he threw up the Nazi salute.

Belloq returned a halfhearted wave.

"You have the artifact?"

"It is here," Belloq said, and patted the canister beneath him. "According to your instructions, it has not yet been sealed. Do you have the payment?"

"First things first," Kroeger said. "I must inspect the merchandise."

Belloq removed the lid of the canister, reached inside, and pulled what looked to Indy like a leather bowling-ball bag from its interior. He started to hand the case to Kroeger, then drew it back.

"Colonel," Belloq said. "Gloves, please."

Kroeger gave a snort of disgust, but withdrew a pair of leather gloves from the pocket of his uniform and slipped them on. Then he took the case from Belloq, unzipped it, and with a gloved right hand removed the Crystal Skull.

"I did not expect it to be so beautiful," Kroeger said. "It is magnificent. Look how it captures the light!"

Kroeger held the skull aloft.

Indy—and the others—caught their breath. Even in the weak glow of the electric bulbs an unholy rainbow of secondary colors burst forth from deep within the skull, shimmering above their heads. The bluish glow of the corona effect, caused by static electricity, danced down Kroeger's sleeve to his shoulder.

As Kroeger turned the skull on his outstretched—and gloved—palm, its vacant eye sockets seemed to skewer all who returned its gaze.

"What power is reputed to lie within this thing?" Kroeger asked. "What makes it so special that men are willing to risk their lives and their reputations to possess it?"

"I have been asking that very question," Belloq said.

Indy's palms became damp. He remembered the first and only time he had touched the skull with his bare hands, how the skull had seemed to throb in time to his heart. Indy was close enough to Kroeger to reach out and snatch the skull. . . .

"The chancellor will be well pleased," Kroeger said, and plunged the skull back into its leather case. "Even if its power is based on mere superstition, it is an unparalleled work of art that will become an inspiration to those of us who have sworn fidelity to the point of death and beyond."

The cavern seemed infinitely darker now.

After handing the case back to Belloq, who gently returned it to the interior of the canister, the colonel removed his gloves and snapped his fingers. Two sailors struggled with a case from the deck of the *U-357*.

They placed the case at Belloq's feet.

"Aren't you going to inspect it?" Kroeger asked.

"I trust you," Belloq said. "But then, I must. What could I do if it were ingots of lead instead of gold? You could blow this cavern to bits, and Malevil above it."

"We could," Kroeger said. "But we won't."

"Merci," Belloq said humorlessly.

"But we do insist that you retire now from your shadowy activities," Kroeger said. "You have made your fortune. Be well satisfied, and avoid the temptation to accept work from our competitors."

"But *mon ami*," Belloq protested. "This was not part of the bargain. I am an archaeologist. It is not a matter of money, but of passion."

"Ah, passion," Kroeger said wistfully. "The weakness of the non-Aryan races. The French, I understand, are particularly susceptible to meaningless sentimentality. How difficult it must be to live with such a handicap."

"You've got to be kidding," Indy blurted out. "Who *are* you guys?"

Kroeger looked at Indy as if he had just noticed him for the first time. He stepped forward and peered at Indy with piercing blue eyes that squinted against the smoke curling up from the cigarette dangling at the corner of his mouth.

Kroeger placed a hand beneath Indy's chin and held his face toward the light, inspecting the recent work of the Daguerre twins. His thumb paused at the scar on Indy's chin left so many years ago by a bullwhip.

"Who is this wretched creature?"

"The name is Jones."

Indy grabbed Kroeger's wrist.

With a flourish, the sailors on either side of Belloq leveled their submachine guns. The Daguerre twins drew their guns at the same time, and Belloq cringed in the middle.

Belloq began to laugh, if unconvincingly.

"He is nobody," the Frenchman said nonchalantly. "A fool...An American tourist who stumbled into the cavern quite by accident. As you can see, my men have already taken care of him."

"Too bad they did not pay more attention to his tongue," Kroeger said, and motioned for his men to lower their weapons. "Jones...such a pedestrian name, no?"

"I do a lot of walking," Indy said.

Kroeger lifted the flap of Indy's holster and withdrew the Webley. "Do American tourists always go abroad armed, Herr Jones?"

"*Doctor* Jones," Indy said. "I'm a college professor. Princeton. And by the way, that thing isn't loaded—I get uncomfortable in a foreign city, and I carry it just in case I need to scare somebody."

"Is that so?" Kroeger asked. He placed the Webley firmly against Indy's temple. He pulled the trigger. The hammer fell with a metallic *snap!*

"Ah, I see that you are correct." Kroeger laughed.

"There is no need to waste your time on this one," Belloq said quickly. "He is really quite harmless."

"Quite," Indy said. "Say, I thought all of these old U-boats were destroyed according to the Treaty of Versailles, but looks like they missed this one." He slowly took the revolver from Kroeger and returned it to the holster. "But I guess you guys have been too busy persecuting Jews, closing down newspapers, and abolishing trial by jury. Huh, Major?"

"Colonel," Kroeger corrected, then bit his lip. "Clever. I am impressed. But tell me, why do you enjoy flirting with death?"

"It beats burning books on a Saturday night."

"You Americans amuse me," Kroeger said. "Everything is a joke to you, and you denounce what you do not understand. Wait, let me tell *you* one. It's about an American who was at the wrong place at the wrong time, and his overly sentimental French friend is unable to save him. Hilarious. Oh, I'm sorry, you look as if you've already heard it."

"Belloq is nobody's friend," Indy said.

"Is this true, René?" Kroeger asked. "You have no association with this man, no connection of any sort?"

"None." Belloq shrugged.

"Then you won't mind killing him," Kroeger said. He relieved one of the sailors of his submachine gun and placed it in Belloq's hands. "You may keep the weapon, as a souvenir of your service to the Third Reich. And do not be surprised if you receive, from time to time, a reminder of your obligation to the Fatherland."

Kroeger snapped his fingers and the sailors lifted the yellow canister between them and carried it carefully toward the *U-357*. The colonel followed, stepping from the flagstones onto the submerged deck of the submarine, then paused.

"I am sorry we did not get to know one another better. But I do not have the luxury of time, since the tide will soon be going out and I have no desire to ground this boat in French territorial waters. *Auf Wiedersehen, Doktor Jones.*"

In a moment Kroeger had slipped down into the conning tower and dogged the hatch behind him. The submarine was already in motion. The con slid deeper into the water as the boat backed out of the cavern toward the subterranean passage to the open sea.

"I could come to hate those guys," Indy mused.

Belloq tossed the submarine gun to Claude, the nearest of the Daguerre twins.

"Surely you're not going to kill me," Indy said, and showed Belloq his empty palms. "The Nazis are gone. There's nobody here but us. I thought we were *friends*. What about all that talk of working together someday?"

"Impossible," Belloq said. "If I do not kill you, they will kill me. In the measure of things, Dr. Jones, it is a small price to pay for my peace of mind."

Claude Daguerre jabbed the snout of the submachine gun in Indy's direction and pulled the trigger, but nothing happened. Jean stepped forward and attempted to wrest the gun from his brother. Belloq cursed them in French to find the safety, but Indy was already scrambling toward the water. He snatched his hat and bullwhip from Belloq's feet at the same time as he heard the clink of the safety.

The cavern erupted in the chatter of gunfire and the whine of ricochets as the submachine gun, the object of a tug-of-war between the Daguerre twins, came to life. Belloq was screaming in French at the twins to take better aim, that any respectable Chicago gangster would know how to handle a fully automatic weapon, so why couldn't they?

Indy jammed his hat tightly onto his head, filled his lungs, and dove into the black water. Bullets zipped around him, strings of bubbles marking their trajectories like aquatic tracers. He felt one of the slugs sting his thigh, but he resisted the urge to grasp the wound and instead swam with all of his might after the slowly retreating submarine. In the dim glow of the running lights he could see the silhouette of the deck gun, and as he reached it he lashed his whip tightly around the muzzle.

He could feel the rhythmic thrum of the screws as the submarine negotiated the passage, and the harsh grating of metal against rock made his heart beat a little faster. The pressure in his ears increased to a painful level as the submarine dove deeper. Indy risked freeing one of his hands from the muzzle of the gun. By pinching his nose and blowing gently, he forced air into the tiny eustachian tubes in the back of his throat. There was a crinkling sound in his ears as the pressure equalized, and the pain disappeared.

His chest, however, felt like fire.

The carbon dioxide building in his lungs was pleading for release. He knew from experience that, for him, this sensation came at a minute and a half underwater. He opened his mouth and let a little of the spent air escape from his lips, which eased the fire somewhat, buying him a little more time. Professional skin divers could hold their breath for four minutes or more, but Indy knew that his own limit was well below that. He had, at best, another ninety seconds. If the U-boat had not cleared the passage into the harbor by the end of that time, Indy knew he would drown.

Indy shut his eyes and forced his mind to go elsewhere, to disengage from his tortured lungs and throbbing brain, to green fields and sunlit pastures. Then the pale blue eyes of Alecia Dunstin popped into his mind, and he studied the waves of her hair, the curve of her jaw, the fullness of her lips. He remembered their first meeting at the British Museum in London, while he stood in front of her desk with hat in hand as she seemed to reach down to his very soul with those remarkable blue eyes. If he drowned, he thought, he would have only one regret.

Then the beat of the props increased and the drag of water against his body stiffened. The submarine had cleared the passage. Indy unlashed himself from the gun. He felt the deck of the submarine slide at an angle beneath his feet as it executed a lazy turn to point the bow seaward.

Indy kicked off his shoes and made for air. The U-boat had only been at ten meters, and in a moment Indy popped to the surface. He gulped in a few lungfuls of fresh night air, got his bearings, then swam toward shore—all the while mentally cursing René Belloq.

Alecia Dunstin had mentally cursed Indy for the hour she had waited on the rock outside the entrance to the ruins of Forteresse Malevil, cursed him for not letting her accompany him into the depths of the cavern. When she had grown tired of cursing him, she made her way down to a café on the waterfront, drank coffee, looked at the full moon overhead, and waited some more.

Finally, she had begun to worry.

She was more relieved than surprised when she saw Indy swimming toward the shore, and she left her table and picked her way around to the shoreline at the base of the fortress. She waded out and met him in waist-deep water, and she threw his left arm around her neck as she helped him up the rocky bank.

Indy coughed and sputtered and sat down on the nearest boulder. He allowed his head to hang between his knees until the coughing subsided. Then he wiped his mouth with the back of his hand and looked up at her.

"It got away," Indy said dejectedly.

Alecia sat down next to him and placed a hand on his leg. When Indy grimaced, she drew her hand away and was shocked to see that it was covered in blood.

"You're injured," she said.

"Shot," Indy said.

"My God," Alecia said. "Let's get you to a doctor."

"No." Indy felt the wound with tentative fingertips. "Most of the force was absorbed by the water. I can feel the bullet just under the skin. I can dig it out with a knife, I think."

"I still think we should get you to a doctor," she

said. "Or a chemist, at least. That could become septic quite easily, you know."

"I'll live," Indy said.

"How did you get out here in the bay?" Alecia asked.

"I hitched a ride on a German submarine. Belloq sold the skull to the Nazis. There, you can still see the wake of the U-boat in the moonlight. It's running shallow, and if you look sharp, you can see the periscope and radio aerials bristling above the water."

"It looks like it's stopped," Alecia said.

"Um." Indy took out his pocketknife and slit open his pants leg to better inspect his wound. "I wish they'd sink. Do you know Belloq tried to kill me?"

"Of course," Alecia said. "Indy, I've been thinking. Maybe all of this business about a curse really is nonsense. Let's just pretend it never existed and stop this foolishness of trying to chase it down. Let the skull go."

"We've tried that already," Indy said.

"Don't pick at that," she said sternly. "That knife's not sterile."

She put her hand beneath his chin and lifted his face to hers.

"You're going to get yourself into a jam you can't get out of one of these days. A bullet that's too deep, or a beating that's too severe, or any one of a hundred other horrible things."

"Alecia, I almost had it," Indy said. "I was close enough to put my hands on it this time. But that submarine can't take it all the way to Berlin, and somewhere along the line there will be another chance—another chance at our life *together*."

"This is driving us both mad," Alecia said. "And we're doing it to ourselves. So let's approach this empirically. The hypothesis is that you are cursed to kill what you love, so let's put it to one last test. Show me how you feel."

"I can't," Indy said.

"Try," she said. "We're alone."

"But all the other times," Indy protested.

"Coincidence," Alecia said.

She leaned forward and allowed her lips to brush against his.

"What's wrong?" she asked. "Don't believe in the scientific method?"

"God help us," Indy said.

He took her in his arms and kissed her. The kiss had in it the force of a passion that had been denied for long summer months that seemed like aeons, a forbidden longing that had threatened to drive both of them mad.

"Now say it," Alecia said as she tore herself breathlessly away.

"You know how I feel."

"Say it, damn you."

Indy caught his breath.

"Alecia Dunstin," Indy said, "I luh—"

"Uh-oh," Alecia said.

She was looking over his shoulder toward the harbor. Indy turned. Far out, but closing fast, a pair of luminous tentacles were reaching toward them in the moonlight.

"Torpedoes," Indy said.

The furious counterrotating screws driving the pair of German self-propelled torpedoes were churning up bioluminescent plankton as they streaked across the harbor toward the base of the old fortress.

"So much for the scientific method," Indy said as he jerked Alecia to her feet.

They scrambled up the rocky slope, and when Indy saw that the torpedoes had nearly run their course, he ducked behind the biggest rock he could find and pulled Alecia down with him. But when the expected explosions did not come, Indy dared a glance over the top and saw that the wakes of the torpedoes had disappeared beneath the ancient fortress.

"They can't both be duds," Indy said.

As if in answer, the *whum-whump!* of a double explosion shook the fortress. Indy felt the power of the blasts reverberate deep in his gut, and he held Alecia tight until the rumbling subsided. When the shower of seawater and small stones subsided, Alecia sat up with a stunned look on her face.

"They couldn't have been aiming at us," she said. "Could they?"

"No," Indy said. "Just a reminder for Belloq. But if we had stayed down there and continued our— *experiment*—the concussion would have killed us both."

The explosion had lured a gaggle of tourists from the cafés and shops surrounding the Old Harbor to the ramparts enclosing Forteresse Malevil. They leaned far out and pointed at Indy and Alecia, chattering excitedly, and one of them thumbed through her phrase book.

"Don't talk to him," her husband said in a thick Chicago accent. "He looks like a bum."

"I'm going to ask him if he's hurt," the woman insisted. "*Ooh ahvay-voo maul?*"

"We're all right," Indy called back.

"What happened?"

"The gas tank of our fishing boat exploded," Indy said. "I guess I shouldn't have been smoking around it. But we're not hurt, at least not badly. Thanks for asking."

"See there?" the woman said. "He speaks pretty good American for a bum."

"They all do," the man said. "It just proves they understand you, even when they stand flat-footed and stare at you like you were from the goddamn moon. Come on, Edith. I know drunken bums when I see them. Probably wasn't even their boat. Throw them some change and let's go."

The woman opened her purse and tossed a handful of coins over the battlement. The coins jingled upon the rocks between Indy and Alecia. Then the American tourists left without looking back, and the crowd dispersed.

"Why do people always throw coins toward me at times like this?" Indy mused.

"Well," Alecia said, brushing herself off and trying to regain her composure. She picked up a fifty-centime piece and stared at it.

On her cheek, a single tear glistened in the moonlight.

"Look at it this way," Indy said, wiping the tear away with his thumb. "We're a little richer. We know the scientific method works. And if we had been killed, at least we'd have died happy."

"But Indiana," she whispered. "That's the problem. I don't *want* to die. I'm sorry, but I can't do this anymore."

1

Dragon Bones

Princeton, New Jersey
Halloween 1933

Alone in his tiny office on the fourth floor of the Department of Art and Archaeology, Indiana Jones unscrewed the bottle of Scotch and regarded with contempt the pile of student papers and unanswered mail on his desk.

Outside, happy ghouls and goblins raced across the quad in search of new victims. But Indiana Jones's door was locked. He had even disconnected his telephone. He had a bellyful of superstition and did not want to be reminded that his belief in science remained unreconciled to his own bitter experience.

It had been a week since he felt like working, and

as the stack of papers grew, the less he was inclined even to begin. Dragging himself to class every day had become an unendurable chore, and he had curtailed many of his lectures and substituted instead heavy reading assignments and guest lecturers. His students would have had cause for concern if his chief pinch hitter had not been Marcus Brody of the American Museum of Natural History.

Indy's routine now pivoted upon the arrival of the daily mail. Only then, as department secretary Penelope Angstrom handed him a new bundle each morning, did a glimmer of hope beat within his chest. Asking Miss Angstrom to shut the door on her way out, he would sort slowly through the letters without opening them. When he had finished he would sort through them again. Invariably, none were postmarked London.

The bottle of Scotch was the latest addition.

He had carried it back to his office and shut himself in this evening on the pretense of attempting to jump-start his flagging work ethic. He allowed himself a crooked smile as he imagined how his father, Professor Henry Jones, would react to this unpardonable breach of trust between a teacher and his pupils.

He poured some Scotch, swished the smoky liquid around in the glass, then raised it in a mock toast.

"Here's to you, Alecia," Indy said. "Or at least, your memory."

As he closed his eyes and brought the glass to his lips, there came a knock that was so soft that Indy was not sure that anyone was at the door. He paused, with the glass beneath his chin, and when the knock came again he shouted that the department was closed.

"I'm sorry," came a female voice. "But I'm looking for Dr. Jones."

Indy was relieved. Princeton was not coeducational, so it could not be a student seeking him out to demand what had become of this paper or that.

"Just a moment," he said, smoothing his hair and straightening his tie. He had almost made it to the door when he remembered the Scotch. He bounded back to his desk, recapped the bottle, and searched frantically for a place to hide it. Not a single desk drawer or file cabinet had enough space left. So he placed the bottle on the floor beside his chair, then snatched up the glass. He began to pour it into a potted plant beside the door, then stopped for fear it would kill the plant. In frustration, he tossed the contents down his throat and slammed the glass back onto the desktop.

"I'm Jones," Indy sputtered as he swung open the door. Then he coughed and wiped his mouth with the back of his hand.

Before him stood a woman in her middle to late twenties in a nun's habit. She stood stiffly, and her hands were folded over a paper sack in front of her. On the fourth finger of her left hand shone a golden band. At first Indy thought the habit was a Halloween costume, a prank that had been engineered to lift his spirits by one of his colleagues.

"Sorry, I don't have anything for your sack."

"I beg your pardon?"

When Indy saw the well-worn rosary that hung at her side, he knew he had made a serious mistake.

"I'm sorry," Indy said. "What can I do for you, Sister?"

"I apologize for disturbing you," she said. "I went to your home but found it dark, so I took the chance that you might be working late. I hope I am not imposing."

"Not at all," Indy said, feeling as if he were back in school. "That is, as long as you're not going to make me recite my Latin. Please, come in."

Indy removed a stack of books from a wooden chair and offered her a seat. When he returned to his own seat behind the desk, he inadvertently kicked the bottle of Scotch. It rolled beneath the desk and toward the center of the room.

"My name is Sister Joan," she said as the bottle came to rest at her feet. She picked it up and regarded the label. "Still celebrating the end of Prohibition? Personally, I could never stand the taste of this stuff—it was always like trying to swallow liquid smoke."

"It's not what you think," Indy said with a lopsided grin.

"Of course not," she replied, trying to find space on the desk to place the bottle. "Even the Lord enjoyed a bit of wine now and again."

Indy took the bottle from her and placed it on the windowsill behind him.

"Pardon me for intruding like this," Joan said. "I know of your reputation, and I have come here for help."

"Go on," Indy said.

Joan eyed him suspiciously.

"First, you should know that I'm being followed. Two cloaked figures dogged my trail to the very steps of this building, and I suspect they are still waiting outside. If you agree to help me, you may be placing yourself at a significant degree of personal risk."

"This is Halloween, Sister," Indy said. "There are people running about in all sorts of weird costumes."

"Yes, but these two men have been following me for more than a week. They ransacked my father's home in Connecticut, and I'm afraid they seriously injured our gardener when he got in the way. Broken ribs and a dislocated shoulder."

"Why would they do that?"

"I don't know," Joan said. "You see, Dr. Jones, my father and I believe in the basic goodness of humanity. Such acts are impossible for me to comprehend. But it may have something to do with what I have in this sack, and because my father is Angus Starbuck."

"The paleontologist."

Indy could feel his head beginning to clear.

"Do you know him?"

"Of course. I met him while waiting for a train in Shanghai, and we passed a delightful hour talking about the dinosaur statues in Central Park. How is he?"

"Lost," Joan said. "Somewhere in the Gobi Desert. That is where this fossil came from, and it is what lured him to such a remote and dangerous land."

She opened the sack and withdrew an oddly shaped horn.

Indy took his glasses from his jacket pocket as Joan handed him the horn. It was more than a foot long, and nearly as broad at the base.

"Remarkable," he said as he studied it beneath the light of the desk lamp. He rummaged in a desk drawer for a magnifying glass.

"Tell me more about your father. When did he disappear?"

"Six months ago," Joan said. "The last letter I received from him was mailed from a place called Urga, in Mongolia."

"Outer Mongolia has been in a tug-of-war be-tween the Russians and the Chinese for decades," Indy said. "Since the Communists took over in twenty-one, all foreigners have been suspected of be-ing spies or saboteurs or worse. It is a difficult place to travel. Six months between letters could be consid-ered normal for that part of the world."

"Or perhaps some warlord is torturing him for the location of more of these bones," Joan said. "The Chinese call dinosaur fossils 'dragon bones' and believe they have magical powers. Taken pow-dered, they are purported to cure everything from the common cold to lack of vitality in men. A cache of these fossils would be worth a fortune on the black market, Dr. Jones."

"Possibly," Indy said. "But it seems unlikely, Sister. You are mistaken about the nature of this piece. It's not a fossil."

"What do you mean?"

"It's not petrified. Bone gets preserved for many millions of years because of minerals that soak into the pores and gradually replicate the original in pre-cise detail. But this specimen shows none of the characteristics of petrification; it is much too light and much too soft for that."

"So it's a fraud?"

"It's from a living animal," Indy said.

"What kind of animal?"

"I'm an archaeologist, not a zoologist. It would

take an expert to say with any degree of certainty. But it would be my guess that it is from a rhinoceros."

"Then why would it excite my father so?"

"I don't know. But we can ask a friend of mine at the American Museum of Natural History. Tomorrow is Saturday, so I have no classes. Would you mind taking the train to New York with me in the morning?"

"Then you will help me?"

"With the bone, yes. In the meantime let's hope that a letter from your father is in the morning post. I think you'll find that we can solve this mystery in short order."

Joan nodded.

"Do you have a place to stay for the night?"

"I'm sure the Young Women's Christian Association will have adequate accommodations," she said cheerfully, although her eyes glanced away. "I believe it is just a few blocks down the street, and I'm sure a brisk walk will do me good."

"Sister, you look beat," Indy said. "Would you consider staying with a friend of mine tonight? Penelope Angstrom is our department secretary and I'm sure she would enjoy the company. Please allow me to telephone on your behalf, and if Miss Angstrom is agreeable, I'll take you over myself."

Joan blushed.

"Yes, of course," she said. "Pardon me, but for a

moment I thought you were going to ask me to stay the night with you."

"It had crossed my mind."

"*Dr. Jones!* You're drunker than I thought."

"I meant because you thought you'd been followed, of course, and because of that business with your father's gardener," Indy said. "Believe me, Sister, I'd sooner cross a rattlesnake than make a pass at a nun."

"What a blunt way to put it," Joan said. "But I'm afraid you're just being honest. Most men, it seems, share your disdain."

"You sound disappointed."

"Frankly, it's one aspect of the calling that I have not quite reconciled myself to." She paused, horrified at what she had just said. "Don't misunderstand me, Dr. Jones. I meant that most men treat nuns as if we're made out of plaster and paint instead of flesh and blood. I have never...I mean, you mustn't think badly of me."

"If you won't call me a drunk, I won't call you a—"

"Understood," Joan said quickly.

Indy wanted to ask her exactly what kind of order she belonged to, but decided to wait for a better time. Instead, he picked up the receiver and jiggled the cradle, attempting to summon the operator.

"I think you must reattach the cord for it to work."

Indy grinned as he replaced the wires in the brass terminals and snugged down the nuts.

"May I ask you a question, Dr. Jones?"

"Shoot."

"You don't seem like the kind of man who would lock himself in his office with a bottle of hard liquor. What kind of demons have you been wrestling with?"

"Demons," Indy said, "That's a good choice of words."

But he did not explain.

"You know what, Sister?" Indy asked as he opened the window. "I've never really liked the taste of this stuff." He opened the bottle, held it outside, and let the contents gurgle onto the grass four stories below.

Suspended from the ceiling of the third-floor gallery of the American Museum of Natural History was a life-size model of a blue whale, made of angle iron and basswood and papier-mâché. The seventy-six-foot model was frozen in the act of diving from the third-floor gallery (Mammals of the World), down through a huge well that opened onto the second floor (Mammals of North America).

Joan paused and stared up, as tens of thousands

of visitors had before her, at the massive bulk of the blue whale looming overhead.

"The biggest animal that has ever lived," she remarked in amazement. "Larger even than the dinosaurs. And they feed almost entirely on plankton, which is microscopic. What a triumph for us mammals."

"I like mammals as well as the next guy," Indy said, pulling her by her elbow. "But if we spend any more time on this floor, they're going to catalog *us*."

"At least we're in the right section," Joan said. She was clutching the paper sack that held the horn.

"Come on," Indy said. "Brody is waiting. There will be plenty of time to visit your cousins later."

A few minutes later they were sitting in Marcus Brody's office on the fifth floor of the museum. While Joan related her story Brody turned the horn over and over in his hands, and ran his fingers repeatedly over the tip. The richly decorated office was as quiet as a tomb, and Indy found himself dozing off in the comfortable leather chair.

"Indy, wake up," Brody admonished when the story was finished. "You're being rude."

"Sorry."

"Don't make him apologize," Joan said. "I'm afraid he has an exaggerated notion of chivalry. He spent the night outside, in his car, protecting me from armies of goblins."

"What a chivalrous fellow," Brody said, placing the horn on the desk. "Reason enough to excuse him just this once. Indy, would you care for some coffee? That should perk you up."

Indy nodded.

"Sister? Would you care for anything? Tea, perhaps?"

Joan shook her head.

Brody touched the intercom on his desk and asked his new assistant to bring coffee for two.

"Well," Joan said. "What do you think?"

"The horn? I'm not sure," Brody said. "I am inclined to agree with Indy's assessment, but let's get an expert opinion, shall we?"

A few minutes later Brody's assistant delivered the coffee tray. The assistant was a brooding young man of twenty-something with closely cropped hair and a complexion turned pale from too much studying and too little sunlight.

"Indy," Brody said. "You should become acquainted with this young man. He's a doctoral candidate at Columbia, and he's working here part-time to pay for his room and board. He's also my nephew. His name is James Brody, although the family calls him Sunny Jim."

"Uncle," the young man pleaded.

"Sorry, James. Ahem. I would like you to meet

Indiana Jones and his friend Sister Joan. Indiana is a professor of archaeology at Princeton, and Sister . . . I'm sorry, what order did you say you were with?"

"I didn't."

"Of course," Brody said.

The young man nodded absently and mumbled some pleasantries.

"Jim!" Brody said. "Can't you be a little more civil?"

"Uncle, I was thinking about something that Joe told me yesterday. He said—"

"Who's Joe?" Indy asked.

"Young Joe Campbell, a Columbia graduate and schoolmaster at the Canterbury School in Connecticut," Brody said. "He has Jim quite under his spell. This Campbell spends his weekends lurking around the museum, hands behind his back, staring for hours at the exhibits, particularly those dealing with American Indians. Frankly, he gives me the creeps. I think he would crawl right up and *become* a part of the exhibits if—"

"What did this Joe have to say yesterday?" Indy inquired, attempting to deflect Brody's rant.

"I'm not sure that I can relate it correctly," James said, suddenly coming to life. "But Joe has been doing a lot of thinking lately about how preliterate societies communicate values through mythology, and how strikingly similar the myths are to one another. It's as if there's only one hero, and one cycle of adventure, and that it keeps getting told over and over again, but with different names and details. Like the Christ story. It doesn't matter if it happened or not—"

"Oh, what rubbish!" Brody exclaimed.

"But Uncle, there you have it," James said. "What matters is the pattern of myth, not the verifiability. Religion turns myth into theology, and that's where we get into trouble. Look how strongly you reacted to the suggestion that the resurrection was not an actual, verifiable event. We have the influence of Western civilization to thank for that."

"And what are we to trust instead?" Brody asked.

"What's in here," James said, and he placed a hand over Brody's heart. "Joe says that recorded history is a nightmare from which we are struggling to awaken."

"That is a quote from *Ulysses,*" Indy said.

"And I suppose we all should throw away our books and turn our backs on the technological wonders of modern science so we can go back to living in grass huts and calling in witch doctors when we're ill," Brody said.

"There you go again, Uncle," James said. "You turn everything into an all-or-nothing proposition. It's clear that you have lost your natural ability to integrate knowledge and spirit."

"Pshaw!" Brody said.

"Actually," Joan said, "I find the idea of recorded history as nightmare compelling, especially considering the most recent chapters—mustard gas, aerial bombing, breadlines, and gangsters. Going back to a more primitive way of life may not be such a bad idea. There would be a certain, well, *innocence* to it."

"And quite a lot of dirt," Brody quipped.

"Don't pay your uncle any mind," Indy said. "These are all things which you'll have to work out for yourself. Besides, I'm sure that when Marcus was your age, he was excited about new ideas, too."

"I'm not ready for the rest home yet," Brody protested. "Look here, Jim, why don't you make yourself useful and run this bone down to the laboratory on the second floor. Ask Dr. Larson to take a look and render us a quick opinion. We will wait. And stay away from that Campbell character, at least for a few days."

"Yes, sir," the young man said, carefully taking the bone.

When James had left, Indy placed his hand on Marcus Brody's shoulder. "You're being too hard on the young man," Indy said. "Give him some slack. The world is still new to him, so let him enjoy it while he can. Besides, there may be something to his friend's ideas, even if the world of Marcus Brody isn't yet ready for them."

"God help me if the world ever is," Brody said. "We can't allow ourselves to give in to these impulses and run willy-nilly over thousands of years of learning and tradition. What would happen to us then?"

"We might just be happy," Joan offered.

"Or unhappy in a way we could not imagine," Brody said. "Pardon me, I am still arguing with my nephew. Indy, you're right. I am too hard on him. You know, Jim's quick mind and strength of will remind me of another young chap I befriended when he was a graduate student many years ago, and he didn't turn out so badly."

Indy grinned.

"It wasn't for lack of trying," he said.

"Well, I like to think my mentoring is what did the trick," Brody said. "By the way, I'm probably acting too much like a meddling uncle with this question, but how are things going with you and your British-librarian friend?"

"You mean Alecia," Indy said. "It's over, Marcus. At least until I can find the Crystal Skull and return it to where it belongs."

"I'm sorry," Brody said.

"She ended the relationship for health reasons," Indy said sadly. "You know I don't believe in curses, but this one—that I will kill what I love unless I return the skull—seems to be working. I can't say that I blame her, Marcus, but it doesn't make it any easier—"

The phone on Brody's desk jangled.

"Ah, it looks as if we have an opinion from the good doctor," Brody said, and picked up the receiver. As he listened his expression grew serious. He searched his pockets for a pen and a scrap of paper, and he jotted down some notes. Brody asked, "Are you absolutely sure?" then replaced the receiver and sat down behind his desk.

"That was Larson," he said.

"And?"

"The bone is from a recently living animal." He looked at his notes. "Larson estimates it has been dead for only a matter of months."

"That's what we thought, isn't it?" Indy asked.

"Well, no," Brody said. "I mean—and this is Larson's expert opinion—that the horn is from a triceratops. That is an animal of the Cretaceous Period, which ended sixty-three million years ago. A *dinosaur.*"

Indy spilled his coffee.

"Is he sure?" Joan asked.

"There is still much to be done, experiments to perform," Brody said. "It is possible that it is some kind of freak of nature, a kind of cosmic practical joke. But Larson is beside himself. He wants us to come right down, and he wants to talk to Sister Joan about the origin of the horn."

Indy dabbed at the coffee stain on his trousers with his handkerchief.

"If it is authentic," he said, "then it could be the most important scientific discovery of all time."

"And we have it." Brody was beaming. "That is, if Sister Joan would be so kind to loan it to us...I promise we will take excellent care of it and give credit where it is due."

"Certainly," she said. "I must admit, however, that it is all rather hard to believe. And you must remember that my chief concern in all of this remains locating my father."

"Your father? But yes, of course," Brody said.

"Marcus," Indy said softly.

"What is it, Indy?"

Indy rose from his chair and walked over to the window. He shoved his hands in his pockets and gazed eastward through the glass, across Central Park and beyond.

"That bone may merely be the prelude to the biggest scientific discovery of all time," he said. "Somewhere out there, there may be a living triceratops that's missing one of its horns. And even if that animal is dead, there may be others.... Marcus, there may be an entire herd of dinosaurs in Outer Mongolia just waiting for us to discover."

Brody caught his breath.

"You can gather all this from an artifact?" Joan asked.

"No, it's not an artifact," Indy said. "Artifacts are man-made. This is an ecofact, a product of nature. And yes, if the horn is indeed genuine, it could prove to be the Rosetta stone of paleontology. It could lead us to the answers to questions that have gripped our imagination since Sir Richard Owen coined the word *dinosaur* a century ago. Only, we'd have to invent a new word for the study of living dinosaurs."

"Then I gather that locating my father has suddenly assumed some added significance," Joan said.

"And urgency," Brody added. He reached behind him and pulled down a color map of Asia. "This may make the search for Dr. Livingstone seem like a walk around the park...."

"So the museum will launch an expedition?" Joan asked.

"The museum isn't capable of financing a full-blown expedition," Indy protested. "In fact, using museum money for expeditions or fieldwork has been strictly forbidden for the last two years. That's why Marcus has relied on my one-man procural service to keep the collections up to date."

"That's true," Brody said. "The Depression has hit the museum as hard as any other institution, and it is unfortunate that so much museum money was tied up in railroad bonds. . . . But Indy, this is different. I'm sure that I can convince the old man that this is a once-in-a-lifetime opportunity."

"The old man?" Joan asked.

"Also, I'm certain that we can rely on private investors."

"Henry Fairfield Osborn," Indy explained. "The museum's president since 1908. If he would agree to fund an expedition to anywhere in the world, Mongolia would be it. For years now he has had a pet theory that humanity evolved in Central Asia, and that the earliest human fossils would be found there."

"The missing link?"

"Something like that," Indy said.

"But we must keep our real reasons a closely guarded secret," Brody continued. "We don't want to have half the world trying to beat us there."

"But Mongolia, Marcus. Think of the difficulty."

"Yes, I know," Brody said, and with his forefinger traced a line from Shanghai in toward the heart of Asia. "An expedition would face some of the harshest conditions on the planet. Temperatures that roast you during the day and freeze you at night. Violent storms and bloodthirsty warlords, and maps that are next to useless. We might as well be launching a journey to the dark side of the moon, so little do we know of the interior. And that's not even considering the attitude of the Russian-controlled government of Mongolia. But then, I didn't say it would be easy."

"You never do," Indy said.

"Well, you wouldn't expect the last living dinosaur to be stamping around some cornfield in Kansas, would you?" Brody lifted the receiver and jiggled the switch hook. "You two go on down and chat with Larson. I'm going to start putting together your expedition."

"My expedition?" Indy asked. "I'm in the middle of a term. I can't leave. Think of the logistics involved—we need trucks and camels and equipment. And that's assuming that the Chinese and the Russians and the Mongols will even let us into the country."

"Indy," Brody said. "We have this one shining chance. Your students can wait. But perhaps there is a living, breathing dinosaur somewhere in Mongolia that cannot."

Dr. Jonathan Larson took a gulp from a beaker of grain alcohol and stared intently at the horn. Then he cleaned his glasses with his shirttail, closed his eyes tightly for a few moments, and snapped them open.

"I keep expecting it to disappear," he told Indy. "I'm still not convinced that I'm not asleep in bed, having a most astounding dream."

"This is no dream," Indy said.

"Are you certain that it's authentic?" Joan asked.

"As certain as anyone can be," Larson said. "We

have no type specimen to work from, but it matches in every respect the fossil horns we do have. It is without a doubt from a triceratops and not a rhinoceros."

"Can you tell anything about the age or health of the animal?" Indy asked.

"Some," Larson said. "The tip of the horn, for example, shows the same pattern of wear—from foraging and battle damage, perhaps—that the fossils do, so it would appear to be from a robust specimen. This horn also appears to be from an adult animal, although it is somewhat smaller than many of the fossil pieces. My guess is that it is from a female. But who knows?"

He took another gulp from the beaker.

"This needs to be properly cataloged," Larson said. "First, we need to send it down to photographic. Then we will have to figure out a place to store it."

"You aren't going to put it into one of those awful vats of formaldehyde, are you?" Joan asked.

"No," Larson said. "I imagine the best thing to do would be to store it in one of the coolers in the kitchen and hope one of the cooks doesn't throw it into a stew."

Larson took a wooden specimen box down from a shelf behind him and placed it on the table. Then, with shaking hands, he placed the horn inside and latched the top.

"Would you mind delivering it to photographic?" Larson asked. "I'm afraid I wouldn't trust myself to carry it that far. It's three floors—"

"I know where it is," Indy said, and picked up the box.

"Do you mind if I carry it?" Joan asked. "It's the last tangible link I have with my father, and I'm afraid I'm not going to be able to touch it again for a very long time."

Indy nodded his understanding and handed over the case.

"Go easy on that stuff," Indy said as he shut the door to Larson's laboratory. "You may actually need some of it to preserve a specimen other than yourself."

As they exited the elevator at the third floor and strolled along the gallery toward the photographic department, which was adjacent to public education, Indy noticed a pair of Asian men leaning against the railing. They were apparently deep in a discussion about the blue whale. Both wore saffron-colored robes that identified them as Buddhists, and both of their heads were shaved.

Joan was on the outside, nearest the men. As she passed them one gave a quick nod of the head, the kind of abbreviated bow as common in the East as touching the brim of your hat is in the West, and Joan smiled.

The man then reached out and, quick as a snake, snatched the specimen box from her hands.

"Indy!" Joan screamed.

The monk with the box was a blur of fluttering orange as he made his way toward the stairwell.

Indy chased after him, but the other monk planted himself squarely in his path. He assumed a fighting stance and his bare toes gripped the floor like claws.

He bowed, in preparation for combat.

Indy stomped the toes of the monk's forward foot with the heel of a well-polished wing tip. As the monk instinctively picked up the foot with the throbbing toes, Indy kicked his other foot out from beneath him.

Then Indy jumped over him and raced to the stairwell.

The escaping monk was well ahead of him and was taking the steps two at a time. But he apparently ignored a sign placed on the landing between the second and third floors that warned of a wet floor. A janitor who was wearily mopping up after several members of a second-grade class from Brooklyn became ill following the shrunken-heads exhibit watched in bewilderment as the monk sailed past him on the slick floor and crashed unceremoniously into the wall.

The specimen box fell from his hands as the monk landed in a heap on the floor.

Indy slid past the sign as well, his wing tips scrambling to find purchase, and crashed into the wall beside the monk. He made a lunge for the box, but the monk kicked it out of his reach.

"Grab the box!" Indy shouted.

"Me?" the janitor asked.

The monk had Indy in a headlock now and was attempting to twist his chin back over his right shoulder.

"Get him off me," Indy mumbled.

The janitor flailed at the monk with the rag end of the mop.

"Use the other end," Indy suggested.

"What? Oh."

The janitor turned the mop around and swung the handle like a baseball bat at the monk's bald head. The monk released Indy, caught the mop handle in the open palm of his right hand, and jerked it away from the janitor. Then he snapped the mop end off with a blow from the edge of his foot.

The janitor ran away.

Indy grabbed the specimen box, scrambled across the wet floor, and went back up the stairs with it. Brandishing the mop handle, the monk sprang after him.

The monk caught up with Indy at the top of the stairs and struck him squarely between the shoulder blades with the handle. Indy was driven against the gallery rail and the specimen box flew out of his hands and landed beyond reach on the back of the blue whale.

"Well"—Indy grinned—"what are you going to do now?"

"*Hai!*" the monk screamed, and charged at Indy.

Indy ducked.

The monk vaulted over the railing, his arms and legs spinning madly as he sailed through the air like a pole-vaulter. He sank into the back of the whale as the wire mesh buckled, and bits of plaster rained down from the ceiling from the overstressed cable anchors.

The monk plucked up the specimen box and shouted in Mandarin to his partner, who was sitting cross-legged near Joan rubbing his foot. He jumped up and in a limping run made his getaway.

"Get some help. Seal off the museum," Indy shouted as he climbed up on the railing. "And tell Brody I'll buy him a new whale."

Indy jumped onto the back of the blue whale. His right foot drove through the skin. Chunks of plaster trembled down from the ceiling as the cables squealed in protest.

"Didn't think I would do it, did you?" Indy asked his foe.

Two of the cables snapped and the whale listed precariously to starboard. On the second floor, the teacher who was leading the second-grade class could not see the two men on the model's back, and she screamed and pulled the children away as the whale seemed to lurch angrily at them.

The monk smashed a hole with his fist through the papier-mâché and wire mesh and descended with the specimen box into the belly of the beast. Indy followed, and as he dropped inside, a piece of wire sliced into his cheek.

"Drat," Indy said, and gingerly touched his cheek.

Then something scurried over his foot and he shook it away. It was a mouse, one of a family of the pesky rodents that had braved the guy wires to make a secret home in the papier-mâché belly of the whale.

The monk was making his way along the angle-iron keel of the beast toward the mouth. Then another cable separated, and the flukes came crashing down on the second floor, smashing a glass display case.

The rest of the whale settled heavily onto the floor.

The family of mice scurried in every direction.

"Bully!" shouted one of the second-graders.

The monk rolled backward along the keel toward the tail, and Indy grasped him by the collar of his robe.

"Who are you?" he demanded.

The monk clutched the specimen box and stared

at Indy with calm brown eyes. He smiled enigmatically, then apologized in Mandarin, which Indy knew.

"For what?" Indy asked.

The monk pressed his fingers firmly into Indy's solar plexus.

Indy sank to his knees, unable to speak. His right hand gripped the hem of the monk's robe, tearing away an orange-colored swatch.

"It will pass," the monk said.

Then the monk kicked a hole through the belly of the whale and disappeared with the specimen box.

After a few minutes Indy was able to crawl outside. He lay on the floor, attempting to catch his breath. Marcus Brody walked over and stood over him. His arms were crossed as he surveyed the damage to the second floor.

"They got away," Brody said. "With the horn."

"I'm sorry," Indy said.

Brody knelt beside Indy and inspected his cheek.

"There is no time to waste with apologies," he said. "You must leave for Shanghai this afternoon. Can you pack in three hours? I'll call Dr. Morey at Princeton and attempt to explain your absence, and offer to assume your classes until your return. First, though, we need to have a doctor look at your face. It looks as though you need stitches."

"Terrific," Indy said.

A mouse scampered across Indy's badly scuffed wing tips. Then what was left of the blue whale emitted one last tortured squeal of wire and metal and collapsed.

2

SHANGHAI

Shanghai, China
November 7, 1933

"I hate this place," Indy said sourly.

"The hotel or the city?"

"Shanghai," Indy said. "I always get a bad feeling in the pit of my stomach when I'm here, and it's not just indigestion. Some places breed nothing but evil."

They were having breakfast in the restaurant lobby of the Cathay, the hotel where, three years earlier, Noël Coward—during a bout with the flu— had written the play *Private Lives* in less than a week.

"Come now, Jones," Granger said, lighting his pipe and pushing aside his empty breakfast plate.

"What's not to like about the Whore of the Orient? Six million people jowl to arse. Inadequate sanitation and rampant disease. Gangsters, brothels, opium dens. A civil war about to break wide open while the Japanese Imperial Army regularly uses the city for bombing practice. I would think this would appeal to your American sense of adventure, Jones."

"I would appreciate it if you would have a little more respect for the city," Joan said. "Shanghai is also called the Paris of the Orient, and deservedly so. The evil that is here is a product of Western civilization, I'm afraid—not China."

Granger cleared his throat.

"Quite right," he said diplomatically.

Indy pushed his breakfast away and concentrated on his coffee. He was exhausted from spending three days in the cramped confines of an American cargo plane as it hopscotched across the Pacific toward China.

"You had better eat those eggs, Jones," Granger said. "It's the last decent food you'll get for some weeks. There are no Michelin guides or four-star hotels where we're going, my brown-eyed friend."

Walter Granger was an adventurer, big-game hunter, and veteran of several expeditions to Outer Mongolia before the borders were closed to foreigners. In fact, Granger had been a key figure in an American Museum of Natural History expedition to

Mongolia that, in the 1920s, had discovered the very first dinosaur eggs known to science.

Although Granger was graying at the temples, he stood ramrod straight at six-feet, one-inch tall and there wasn't an ounce of fat on his tanned body. His only physical defect was a badly mauled right ear. He was dressed this morning, as he was every morning, in a khaki shirt with loops over the pockets for cartridges. His ever-present bush hat was also khaki, with a leopard-skin band taken from the cat that had chewed off most of his right ear. Granger wore the hat, even indoors, claiming that he could hear better with it on.

But beyond his obvious qualifications—and in spite of his idiosyncrasies—the real reason Granger had been asked to lead the expedition was that Indy trusted him. Years before, Granger had saved him from becoming the main course for a tribe of Polynesian cannibals by convincing them that blue-eyed foreigners were much tastier than the common brown-eyed variety—and setting them on the trail of a notorious Dutch slave trader named Conrad.

The tribe later thanked Granger for the tip.

Granger knocked out his pipe in an ashtray and dropped the stem in one of the cartridge loops over his breast pocket. Then he cleared the middle of the table and unrolled a map, using the salt-and-pepper shakers and Indy's coffee cup to hold down the curling edges.

"I laid out the route this morning while waiting for you to arrive," Granger explained. "It is subject to your approval, Jones, but I think you will agree it makes the most sense. From Shanghai we will travel by rail to Kalgan, where the tracks end at the base of the Shen Shei Mountains. From there, we will take a treacherous stretch of road that serpentines along the cliffs and leads to a gateway in the Great Wall at Wanshan Pass. That's roughly a thousand miles from here."

"Yes, I believe that is the route my father took," Joan said. "He said as much in one of the last letters I received."

"It is the only way in or out," Granger said. "The pass was used by caravans for a thousand years before Marco Polo saw it. . . . After gaining the plateau, we have a three-hundred-mile stretch called Desolation Road to the capital at Urga. There, it will be Indy's job to obtain the necessary permits from the Russian-controlled government. Otherwise, the expedition is over."

"I'll use my charm," Indy quipped.

"If all goes well to that point," Granger said, "we will obtain camels for our caravan from one of the many traders along the Urga Road. Then we will set out toward the west, and penetrate hundreds of miles into the Gobi. The desert is the haystack, and your father, Sister Joan, is the proverbial needle."

"But if luck is with us," Indy said, "we'll have

gathered some clues along the way to guide us in the right direction."

"And if it isn't?" Joan asked.

"Hopeless is not strong enough a word," Granger said.

"Then I will pray for luck," she said.

A young Chinese man entered the restaurant, searched for Granger, came to the table, and handed him a handful of manifests.

"I'd like to introduce you to a rather capable fellow," Granger said. "This is Wu Han, a scholar and jack-of-all-trades who has helped to put the expedition together these last few days. Frankly, I told Brody that I didn't think I could do it. And I couldn't have if it hadn't been for Wu Han here."

Wu Han bowed to Joan, then shook hands with Indy.

"It has been a pleasure to help my American friends," Wu Han said in perfectly accented English. "I only hope that I can continue to be of service. Is this your first time in Shanghai? Perhaps I could arrange some entertainment."

"This is old hat for Dr. Jones," Joan said, "but it's my first time and I could use a bit of relaxation. I hate to miss an opportunity to explore a new city."

"There is plenty to sightsee," Wu Han said. "May I call for you this evening? Perhaps Dr. Jones would like to come as well. I understand from Mr. Granger that he is quite a fan of hot American jazz."

"Jazz?" Indy said. "Well, perhaps."

"Good," Wu Han said. "You may expect me at about six o'clock, if that is convenient. Mr. Granger, sir, is everything in order? May I be excused?"

"Yes, of course," Granger said, glancing over the manifests that Wu Han had brought. "Thank you."

Wu Han bowed.

"Trap you later," he said.

"Catch," Granger barked. "The phrase is 'catch you later.' "

"Of course," Wu Han said.

"Ah," Granger said. "Most of the equipment has been loaded onto the flatcars, with the exception of a special shipment that I had requested from our friends at the British arsenal. We are scheduled to leave at oh-five-hundred, and Brody's instructions made it clear that time is of the essence. No matter how good the jazz is, Indy, I suggest that you get some sleep tonight."

"Sleep." Indy sighed.

"Jones." Granger leaned conspiratorially toward Indy. "Brody's cable made it clear that this expedition's primary objective is to locate Professor Starbuck. But some of the equipment he has required does not seem to be useful, even tangentially. What do we need with several *quarts* of animal tranquilizer? I was prudent enough not to wire him back and ask what was going on, but now that I'm sitting across from you, I feel the time is right. Jones, what in hell is going on?"

"All I can tell you now," Indy said, "is that Brody is right when he says our mission is to locate Professor Starbuck. You're no fool, Granger. But don't ask me anything else until we are safely inside Mongolia."

"Funny pairing of words, that," Granger said.

"What?" Joan asked.

"Safe," he said, "and Mongolia."

Indy traced his finger along the path from Shanghai to Mongolia. Then he spread his hand, bridging the gap from Peking to the Shen Shei Mountains with his thumb and little finger.

"I would have preferred to launch this expedition from Peking," Indy said. "Now, there's a city I like. Clean, beautiful; friendly people. And it's closer to where we're going."

"That would bring us too close to the Japs for comfort," Granger said. "Since they've taken Manchuria—Manchuku, they call it—nothing in the north is safe."

"I'd prefer it if you would call them Japanese," Joan requested.

"Why?" Granger asked. "They call us worse. They have a name for us that means 'big feet and smells like hamburger.' They think even less of the Chinese and Koreans."

"If we are to expect the best from others, we

should demand the best from ourselves," Joan asserted. "Besides, I'm sure that not all the Japanese feel that way."

"I'm sure you have a point, Sister," Granger said. "But I'm glad I won't have to put up with it all the way to the Gobi and back."

"What do you mean?" Joan asked, stiffening.

"You're staying here," Indy said.

"Why, that makes no sense at all," Joan protested. "Neither of you knows my father. You don't even have a recent photograph for reference. What if you overlook some important clue?"

"I'm sorry," Indy said, "but the Gobi is no place for a woman. There are things out there that you can't even begin to imagine."

"How do you know what I can begin to imagine?"

"Well," Indy said. "I just—"

"Look here," Granger interrupted. "Do you know what would happen if one of the local warlords got their hands on you? You'd be sold into white slavery quicker than you could say your Hail Mary, and there would be nothing we could do about it."

"You're not going to scare me into being a good little nun," Joan fumed. "The Catholic Church has been trying to do that for years and it hasn't worked, so why should you two hooligans think you can do it?"

Granger coughed and looked away.

"That must be some order you belong to," Indy said.

"Stop making jokes," Joan said, brushing tears away with the back of her hand. "Oh, I know what you're thinking now—you're thinking how weak I am, and how I cry at the drop of a hat. Well, let me tell you something. I'm not crying for me. I'm crying for *you* two because you're such Neanderthals."

Indy leaned over the map and jabbed his finger into the center of Mongolia.

"Urga," he said. "You go as far as Urga. And that's it."

If the patrons of the Lotus Eaters nightclub knew that Asia was poised on the brink of war, they did not show it. The well-dressed international crowd, Indy thought, was a microcosm of the rest of the world: they drank and dined and danced as if the party would never end.

Joan's habit had not raised a single eyebrow in the exotic cabaret, where the dance floor was crowded with the uniforms and noisy with the tongues of a dozen nations. The only Chinese faces in the crowd were those of the waiters, the jazz band, which tried fiercely but unsuccessfully to capture the Dixieland sound, and the club's proprietor, a round-faced gangster by the name of Lao Che.

Despite Lao's rotund appearance, his hard eyes had a decidedly wolfish gleam.

Indy knew him by reputation, but had never met him.

"This is the busiest nightclub in Shanghai," Wu Han boasted. "All of the best people come here."

"If these are the best," Indy said, "I would hate to see the worst." He had been watching the steady stream of traffic past Lao Che's corner table, and noted with dissatisfaction the amount of money that had crossed the table. Set into the wall behind the table was a locked cabinet that held rows of jars; the majority were of stone, but a few were ornately carved ivory or jade.

"I'm sorry," Wu Han said, crestfallen. "Do you not care for the hot jazz? We could go somewhere else."

"The music is fine," Indy said. "Very good. I didn't mean to hurt your feelings. It's just that what is going on at that table over there makes me very uncomfortable."

Wu Han's face grew serious.

"Lao Che is a very powerful man, Dr. Jones," he said. "It is better to pretend not to notice such activity. He holds Shanghai like this." Wu Han closed the fingers of his right hand into a tight fist. "I apologize if I have offended you by bringing you here."

"There is no need to apologize," Indy said easily.

"We will go," Wu Han said.

"No, of course not," Indy said. "Besides, it is very impolite to walk out when the band is in the middle of a number. We will stay for a few more songs."

"As you wish."

"Did you enjoy your visit to the Bund this evening?" Indy asked.

"Oh, yes," Joan said. "Wu Han is an exceptional guide."

"I agree," Indy said. "As a matter of fact, Wu Han is pretty exceptional at everything he does. He knows instinctively what must be done, and then does it. I don't know what Granger is paying you, but it isn't enough."

Wu Han bowed slightly.

"The honor of working with the great American archaeologist is pay enough," he said. "Also, Joan has been kind enough to correct my poor English."

"Your English is perfect." Joan laughed. "You just need some help with your idioms."

"Pardon my bluntness," Indy said, "but you *are* being paid?"

"My services have been acquired through an arrangement with my employer," Wu Han said.

"Your employer?" Indy asked. "Granger said you were a scholar. Do you teach at the university?"

"No," Wu Han said. "I was a student of political science, but before taking my degree, I was forced to leave for the sake of my honorable family."

"Well, money is sometimes difficult to come by, even for a scholar and a jack-of-all-trades," Indy said. "So you work for a local businessman."

"Yes." Wu Han's face brightened.

"Look," Indy said. "We need someone like you to make this expedition run smoothly, someone to ease the inevitable friction we will meet among the locals. You'll get paid, so you won't have to worry about your family, and when we get back I'll arrange it so that you can finish your studies... in America, perhaps."

Wu Han looked as if Indy had punched him in the stomach.

"What is it?" Joan asked.

"I am undeserving of such a generous offer," Wu Han said. "Although I am very grateful for your confidence in me, I am afraid that it is impossible for me to leave Shanghai."

"There is something you're not telling us," Indy said.

"Duty requires that I fulfill my obligations to my family and to my employer," Wu Han explained. "My prayers, however, will accompany you on your journey."

"This employer," Indy said. "It's Lao Che, isn't it?"

Wu Han was silent.

"What kind of mess are you in?"

"Please, Dr. Jones. You must remember my family."

"Where is your family now?" Joan asked. "Perhaps we can help them, and then you would be free of this gangster."

"Family dead," Wu Han said, his English disintegrating as emotion welled up inside him. "Parents and baby sister die in the influenza epidemic."

"I am sorry," Joan said.

"Do not be," Wu Han said. "It is the cycle of things. We loved each other very much in the time we had."

"But if they are dead," Joan asked, "how is Lao Che controlling you through them? It doesn't make sense."

"He has their souls," Wu Han said softly.

Joan looked puzzled.

"Their ashes," Indy said. "The bastard has their ashes."

"Yes," Wu Han said. "He controls many of my people in this way. We are required to do detestable things, to assist in the enslavement of others through opium and prostitution. I keep his books. But I am ashamed, just the same."

"How long must you work for him for the release of their ashes?"

"Ten years," Wu Han said. "For each individual."

"You'll be in your fifties before you're free," Joan said.

"I have no choice," Wu Han said.

"We're talking about their ashes," Joan said. "Not their souls."

"This is China, Sister," Indy said. "If the dead aren't buried ritualistically in the family plot, then their souls wander the earth, begging for their living relatives to end their anguish."

"That's ridiculous," Joan blurted.

"Is it?" Indy asked. "I'm sure that some of your beliefs seem equally absurd to Wu Han. Only, he's polite enough not to say so."

Joan blushed.

"I'm sorry," she said.

"No," Wu Han said. "I am the one who should apologize, for burdening your carefree evening with my unimportant troubles. Please, forget about all of this. I will show you a different club, where the hot jazz is the cat's nightclothes."

Wu Han stood up.

"Not yet," Indy said.

"You would like to stay?"

"Tell me this," Indy said. "More than anything else, would you like to be free of this dishonorable life and sure that your family will rest in peace? And if this were to happen, you would accompany the expedition and finish your education when we return?"

"Of course, Dr. Jones. But—"

"No buts. And call me Indy."

"Please," Wu Han said. "I cannot break my agreement with Lao Che. I would lose face and dishonor my family. There is nothing I can do. I made a promise."

"*I* didn't make any promises," Indy said. "And if I allowed a friend of mine to be tortured in such a fashion by a drug-dealing, pig-faced, two-bit gangster like Lao Che, I would lose face. Can you understand that?"

"Friend." Wu Han spoke the word reverently.

"Dr. Jones," Joan said. "With all due respect to Wu Han and the remains of his family, I don't think we ought to get involved. Don't you think we should let the authorities handle this?"

"Lao Che probably has the ashes of their ancestors locked up in that little cabinet of his," Indy said. "Wu Han, which of those urns behind him belongs to your family?"

"Third shelf, middle. The stone urn with the characters for peace and prosperity."

"Sister, I'll need your help—if you're game, that is."

"Of course I'm game, as you say. If you truly think we can help Wu Han without getting all of us killed."

"Don't worry," Indy assured. "Odds are they can only kill one of us before the others get away. I'm going to the men's room now, and I am going to act extravagantly drunk. When I get back to the table, I'm going to be in a rather unpleasant mood. So remember, I'm not your friend."

"Not my friend?" Wu Han sounded puzzled.

"We'll be pretending."

"Yes, of course."

When the band reached the end of the number, Indy stood, swayed for a moment, then reached over and took Joan's half-empty glass of wine and finished it. Then he slapped it back down on the table with such force that it tumbled over, rolled to the edge, and broke on the floor.

All eyes turned toward them.

"Sorry," Indy said with a stupid grin and just enough of a slur to be convincing. Then he ambled across the room and backed clumsily into another waiter, whose tray crashed to the floor.

"First night on the job?" Indy asked.

"Please, sir," the waiter said, reaching first for the mess on the floor and then for Indy's elbow. "Won't you let me help you to the—"

Indy shook him off.

"I'm fine," Indy insisted, and continued on.

The band leader glanced worriedly at Indy, then struck up a lively version of "Ain't We Got Fun?"

Once inside the men's room, Indy nodded pleasantly to the attendant who held a basket of hot towels at the ready. Indy walked to the mirror and inspected his hair, then jerked a thumb toward the dance floor. "There's a heckuva mess out there," he said. "A drunk dumped a big tray of drinks on the floor. They can't seem to find the janitor. Maybe you should go help."

The attendant looked uncertain.

"Go on," Indy urged, pretending to admire his own reflection. "My date would like to dance, and we can't with that mess out there." He dug in his pocket and dropped some coins onto the attendant's plate.

The attendant nodded and hurried out.

As soon as the door closed, Indy went to the ash can by the door. Except for one smoldering cigar butt, it was clean—the attendant apparently took his job seriously—and Indy unfolded the handkerchief from the breast pocket of his dinner jacket and laid the square of cloth on the floor. He frowned as he picked up the moist cigar butt with his bare fingers and flung it away. Using both hands, he repeatedly scooped sand from the ashtray into the handkerchief. When he thought he had about the right amount, he tied the corners of the handkerchief together. Just as he was shoving the package into his sock, the attendant returned.

"It is under control, sir," the attendant announced.

"Of course it is," Indy agreed, and left.

Indy repeated his performance with only slightly

diminished vigor on the way back to his table, but he did not sit. "I want you to introduce me to Lao Che," he said as he used both hands to steady himself on the edge of the table.

"But Dr. Jones," Wu Han said. "Perhaps now is not the time."

"Now," Indy insisted, a little louder than necessary.

"As you wish." Wu Han lowered his eyes.

Indy leaned on Wu Han's shoulder as they made their way to the corner table. Joan followed a few steps behind, and with every step berated Indy for his inability to judge his capacity for liquor.

Lao Che was flanked by his three sons. All were from different mothers. There was one fat one, one painfully skinny one, and one that was as handsome as the others were homely. Each, however, had the telltale bulge of a gun hidden beneath his jacket.

In Chinese, Wu Han quickly begged the gangster's pardon and apologized for Indy's vulgar behavior. Lao Che laughed and said that all Americans were fools, so why should this one be any different?

Lao Che seemed only vaguely aware of Wu Han's identity.

"Do you work for me?" Lao Che asked suspiciously in Chinese.

Wu Han replied that he had been assigned to assist with the American expedition, then quickly filled him in on the details.

"I am pleased to meet you, Dr. Jones," Lao Che grunted in English. "I am glad that you are enjoying yourself. May I get you anything more? Or for you, Sister?"

"No, thank you," Joan said. "And I think Dr. Jones has had quite enough. As you can see, he can be quite a handful."

"I'm afraid she's right." Indy grinned.

"Is this your conscience?" Lao Che asked. "Tell me, why does a Catholic sister accompany you? Planning to make some converts upon your arrival in Mongolia, Dr. Jones?"

"I do what I can," Joan said. "One soul at a time."

"As I do!" Lao Che said. "One cannot abandon the spiritual side of life in pursuit of earthly pleasures, eh? And speaking of earthly pleasures, I hope you are not feeling too badly in the morning. Would you like me to send one of my girls home with you to nurse what will soon be an aching head? It is the best hangover remedy I know. I'm sure that the good sister will turn a blind eye to such an act of mercy."

"No thanks, Lao," Indy said. "And if the sister has a blind eye, I've yet to find it."

Lao Che laughed.

"This one—what the devil is his name? I have so many employees that I forget—tells me that everything is in order for your departure," he said. "I hope that you and Mr. Granger have found him to be of some service."

"Yes," Indy said. "He is an excellent employee. You should congratulate yourself on being a good judge of character—and a shrewd businessman."

"It just takes the right incentive," Lao Che said modestly.

"You also seem to be a fine judge of collectibles," Indy continued. "From our table, I couldn't help but admire your collection of funerary vases. Wu Han attempted to discourage me from asking you about it, saying that you would be too modest to discuss them. But I would really like to see them up close."

"They are nothing," Lao Che said.

"Really, they are quite compelling," Indy said, sounding more and more sober. "Even from a distance, I could tell it is a rather complete collection. If you would grant me just a quick examination, I would be most grateful."

Lao Che fingered the key to the cabinet, which hung from a golden chain around his neck.

"Really, Dr. Jones," he said. "Most of them are quite common."

"Where are your manners?" Joan scolded. "Can't you see that you are embarrassing Mr. Che?"

"I wasn't trying to embarrass him," Indy said. "Actually, the museum would be interested in purchasing some of the jars to complete its funerary exhibit. But I can understand how he would be reluctant to part with them."

"Dr. Jones!" Wu Han protested. "Such things are not for sale."

Lao Che smiled broadly.

"Come now," he said. "In the interest of contributing to a museum collection, it is possible I could be persuaded. Which of the urns were you most interested in?"

Lao Che slipped the chain over his head and turned, poised with the key in his hand.

"The jade one on the top shelf," Indy said.

"Some of them still contain ashes, unfortunately," the gangster said as he swung open the cabinet door. "After so much time, who knows who they belong to? But propriety insists that the remains stay here in Shanghai, where they belong, because eventually a descendant may be found."

"Of course," Indy said. "The museum is interested only in the pieces themselves."

Lao Che carefully took down the jade urn and placed it on the table, under the watchful eyes of his sons.

"Exquisite," Indy said. He drew his glasses from his shirt pocket and slipped them onto the bridge of his nose. He bent down so that he would be at eye level with the piece.

"May I?" he asked.

Lao Che hesitated.

"The museum would be willing to offer a handsome price for pieces of this quality," Indy said.

"Please," Lao Che beamed. "Be my guest."

Indy picked up the jar and cradled it in his hands. He brushed his thumbs over the intricate reliefs of hissing dragons and soaring cranes.

"It is Manchu," Lao Che said.

"From the Manchu Dynasty?" Joan asked.

"No," Indy said. "It is a relatively recent piece from the large ethnic group called the Manchus. There are more than fifty such groups in China, each with a separate culture, set of beliefs, and language. That's why there's been an almost constant state of civil war, and why travel and politics are so difficult here. Properly, only the Han are considered true Chinese. But even among the Han there are scores of subgroups, and hundreds of dialects."

"Is there an example of a Han vase?"

"Yes," Indy said, and returned the jade container to Lao Che. "This stone one here in the center. Lao, do you mind?"

The gangster picked up an urn beside the one Indy wanted.

"No," Indy said. "The Han vase, there. Yes."

Lao Che nervously handed over the stone vase. Wu Han sucked in his breath and closed his eyes.

"See how plain this one is?" Indy said, and he held it just below the edge of the table as he showed it to Joan. As he did, Joan leaned over and pretended to inspect it. With his thumb, Indy tapped the pocket of his jacket. Joan tugged upon the pocket with a fore-finger, and in one motion Indy lifted the top from the urn and poured the remains of Wu Han's immediate family into the right pocket of his dinner jacket.

"No ornamentation except for the bold charac-ters for peace and prosperity. Rather simple, don't you think?" Indy held the vase up. "Now, on the bottom here—"

"Dr. Jones!" Joan shouted.

The vase slipped from Indy's fingers and fell to the floor. Indy dove to retrieve it and pulled the handkerchief with the ashtray sand from his sock. He spilled the contents onto the floor around the vase.

"Oh no, look what I've done," Indy said. "It seems I've scattered the remains of some poor devil all over the floor. Here, let me gather it up."

Wu Han nearly passed out, and had to clutch Joan's arm to keep from joining Indy on the floor.

"My sons will clean up the mess," Lao Che said.

"Are you sure?" Indy said, placing the urn on the table and shaking his handkerchief into it. "I think I've got most of it here."

Lao Che's skinny son joined Indy beneath the table while the fat one peered into the urn and made a sound of disgust. With his thumb and forefinger he removed a cigarette butt from the sand.

"Sorry," Indy said, his head bobbing above the table. "Must have come from the floor."

Lao Che grunted.

"Perhaps we should continue this another time," Indy suggested, getting to his feet and patting the sand from his knees. "Maybe when I'm a little more sober than I am right now."

Lao Che stared at Indy in surprise.

"Come along, Dr. Jones," Wu Han said, pulling him by the arm. "Let's get you to bed. The first stage of a very long journey starts in the morning, and you need to be ready."

As they piled into a taxi outside the door of the Lotus Eaters, Indy took off his jacket and handed it to Wu Han. "I believe this," he said, "belongs to you."

The expedition's equipment, loaded onto a trio of flatcars at the railyard adjacent to the docks at Shanghai, looked suspiciously like a military campaign in the predawn light. The item that drew the most attention from the railway workers was the .30-caliber machine gun mounted on the back of one of the three brand-new trucks. The trucks had been donated to the expedition by the Dodge Motor Company, which had supplied the museum with vehicles in the past, but the machine gun had arrived from the British arsenal.

"Really," Joan fumed at Indy as a canvas was secured over the truck and the gun. "Do we need that horrible thing? We're here to find my father, not to start a war."

"Sister," Indy said, his breath hanging in the cold air, "that may amount to the same thing. There are things out there—bandits, warlords, private armies—of which you know absolutely nothing. Things that don't share your belief in the natural goodness of humanity."

Indy looked at his watch. It was four-fifteen.

"Wu Han," he said, and zipped up his leather jacket. "Is there any way we can slip out of here now? I would like us to be on our way well before anyone suspects we've gone."

"It is a freight train," Wu Han said. "There is a timetable. There are things to consider, such as other trains on the same track. But I will try to persuade the engineer."

"Try with this." Indy pressed a wad of bills into Wu's hand.

"Consider it done," Wu Han said.

Granger walked alongside, a clipboard in his hands and his pipe in his mouth, inspecting the flat-cars one last time for everything that was supposed to be on board.

"Let's get rolling," Indy called.

"In time," Granger said. "If we miss anything, there won't be a corner drugstore we can pop into and replace it. Not even Sears and Roebuck reaches this far out."

Indy stepped onto the platform at the back of the passenger car, which was coupled to the last of the expedition's flatcars. He pulled Joan up behind him.

Indy could hear the chugging of the cylinder head of the aging steam locomotive deepen in pitch as the boiler gained pressure.

"This train is moving whether you're on board or not," he called to Granger.

"All right, old man," Granger responded. "Keep your shirt on. I don't know what the rush is; we're not scheduled to leave for another forty-five minutes."

"Call it Yankee ambition," Indy said, and sat down next to Joan on one of the hard-backed wooden seats. As Granger came and sat opposite them the car lurched and the locomotive pulled forward to take the slack out of the line of cars. Then the engineer opened the throttle a couple of notches and the Shanghai railyard began to glide away around them.

"That was a wonderful thing that you did for Wu Han last night," Joan told Indy. Awkwardly, she patted his shoulder through his leather jacket.

"We're not out of Shanghai yet," Indy warned. He lowered the fedora, leaned back against the seat, and closed his eyes. He did not feel well. He was not exactly sick, but he did have a terrible case of indigestion. Joan had insisted on eating a traditional Chinese meal before their visit to the nightclub last night, and Indy was afraid that he had gotten a bad eel. "Let me know when we're safely in the country."

Wu Han stepped down from the locomotive and allowed the train to pass. As the passenger car neared he took a few steps to gain momentum and grabbed the rail, swinging himself up onto the rear platform.

In a Buddhist cemetery at the outskirts of the city, sticks of incense still burned as gaily colored prayer flags fluttered over the remains of his family. Their ashes had been safely entered into a secretly purchased granite vault. When Wu Han's time came, the lid of the vault would be lifted and his ashes would be sprinkled with those of his parents and baby sister.

Wu Han stood for a moment on the platform. A great weight had been lifted from his shoulders. He breathed in great lungsful of air, and he noted, as if for the first time, the aroma of the city: sewage, seawater, wood smoke from the locomotive, and the unmistakable odor of spoiled meat and fish from the nearby open-air market.

"So long, Lao Che," Wu Han said to the wind. "May I never have to breathe your stench again."

* * *

Three hours outside of Shanghai, as the freight high-balled on its ribbon of narrow-gauge rail through an endless quilt of canals and rice paddies, Joan shook Indiana Jones awake.

"Time for breakfast," she said, and placed a cardboard box on his lap.

Indy felt even worse than he had when the train had left. He inspected the contents of the box. Mostly rice, with a little bite of fish rolled up into a large piece of seaweed. Also, a pair of bamboo chopsticks and a rough paper napkin.

The fish smelled a little too much like eel for comfort.

"It's unappetizing," Indy said, and pushed the box aside. "Do we have any coffee?"

"Green tea," Joan said. "There's a pot of it on the brazier in the front of the car. There's also a cooler of water next to it. Aren't you feeling well?"

"I've felt better," Indy replied.

"You were warned about drinking too much last night."

"Very funny." Indy wasn't smiling. "I was just acting, remember?"

"I think you enjoyed it a little too much."

"This is the worst first impression I've ever made," Indy muttered, and worked his way to the aisle. Although the train was slated as a freight, the passenger car had filled with people from a half-dozen stops since leaving Shanghai. All of them

were Chinese, and many of them had their belong-
ings in bundles at their feet. Indy smiled repeatedly
as he made his way to the front of the car, but got no
smiles in return.

He peered into the open top of the battered five-
gallon can that was used as a watercooler. Bugs and
other less identifiable bits of debris were floating in
it. He took a tin cup, rinsed it out with water from
the can, and poured some tea from the kettle that sat
atop the coal-fired brazier.

As he sipped the scalding liquid he looked out
through the dirty glass in the front of the car at the
expedition's equipment. The canvas was in place
and everything was still in order. Then he looked
around idly at the interior of the passenger car, and
decided from its style and its well-worn condition
that it must have been in use since the turn of the
century.

When he looked at the brake system hanging beneath the flatcar ahead as the train rounded a curve,
however, he knew that estimate was overly generous.
Although the train was equipped with air brakes,
they were the older kind, which required the applica-
tion of air pressure, pumped from the locomotive, in
order to work. The newer safety brakes—which had
been in use in America since the 1890s—were de-
signed so that the brakes were applied when air pressure was *lost;* if the system were ruptured or if the

cars became separated from the locomotive, the brakes would automatically engage.

But the only way to brake this train if the system failed would be to manually turn a huge hand wheel at the end of each car.

"Great," Indy said, and spat out a bug.

He dumped the rest of the cup out the window.

"Do you not care for the tea?" Wu Han asked, coming up from behind. "Can I get you something else, Indy? There is a small supply of chocolate bars and American soda loaded onto the flatcars. Would you care for something?"

"Soda?" Indy asked.

"Yes," Wu Han said. "Root beer."

"I would kill for a root beer," Indy said. "My stomach has been queer all morning."

"I could get you some medicine, too."

"No, a root beer is what I need. The carbonation, you know. But the flatcars are secured, and it would be too much trouble. Maybe even dangerous, if you lost your balance."

"No trouble," Wu Han said. "I come from a long line of acrobats. And I know exactly where to look, on the middle car. Just lift the edge of one canvas and there they are."

"I'll go with you." As he spoke, Indy suppressed a murderous belch.

"Sit down," Wu Han said cheerfully. "I'll be back in a spark."

"Flash," Indy corrected. "Back in a flash."

"Of course. Thank you."

Wu Han was suddenly out the door and walking expertly over the cargo. Indy sat down and watched while his young Chinese friend hopped onto the middle car. He paused at the corner of one bundle, unknotted the cord that held the canvas, and pried open the top of one of the crates with his fingers.

"Don't want to arm-wrestle that one," Indy told himself.

Wu Han withdrew two bottles of root beer, then secured the crate and retied the canvas. As Wu Han worked Indy noticed a second figure darting behind the cargo on the flatcar, sneaking up behind him. It was a man, dressed in black, with a knife between his teeth.

"Watch out behind you!" Indy shouted from the open door of the passenger car, but his words were lost in the rush of the wind and the rumble of the train.

Wu Han smiled and held up the bottles of root beer.

The figure had crept to within arm's reach of Wu Han.

Indy opened the door and vaulted onto the platform. He drew the Webley from its holster, then hesitated. The lurching of the train would make aiming difficult. Indy was afraid he would hit Wu Han instead of his assailant.

"Get down!" he shouted.

The assassin had the knife raised in his right hand.

"What?" Wu Han shouted back.

Indy aimed over Wu Han's shoulder and fired.

The bullet struck the assassin in the shoulder, knocking him backward onto the covered hood of one of the Dodge trucks. He scrambled for a secure grip for a moment, then tumbled over the edge of the flatcar onto the roadbed.

Indy crossed the first flatcar and joined Wu Han.

"When you say you would kill for a root beer," Wu Han said, "you weren't kidding."

"Get back to the passenger car," Indy ordered. "There may be more of them out here. Tell Granger that we've got some trouble, and keep Sister Joan inside with her head down."

"Right."

"Wait," Indy said. He took one of the bottles of root beer.

"Bottle opener?"

"Right here," Wu Han said.

Indy flipped off the cap and guzzled down a third of the bottle before Wu Han had made it back to the passenger car. Indy sat down on a cargo box. While he waited, with his gun in his right hand, he finished off the rest of the bottle.

"I love root beer," he announced.

Indy felt a magnificent burp building in the pit of his stomach, and since he was alone on the flatcar, he opened his mouth and allowed nature to take its course. He belched long and loud, and immediately the pressure in his tortured guts subsided.

"Dr. Jones," a voice said in Mandarin as he felt the prick of a knife blade at the back of his neck. "Have you forgotten your manners? But then, I suppose you never had any."

"Did Lao Che send you?"

"Who else?" the voice asked, changing to English with a British accent. "No, don't turn around. The others can't see me and we wouldn't want to alarm them. And careful with that gun—somebody could get hurt, you know. Keep it in your lap."

"You're the boss."

"You couldn't have expected to get away with that little switch routine at the nightclub last night. It was apparent as soon as Lao's oldest son went to the water closet and discovered the ash can had been tampered with."

"I thought it was clever."

"You would," the voice said. "You have a choice. Either you will tell me where Wu Han has hidden the remains of his family so that Lao Che can restore his contract, or I will kill you first and Wu Han second."

"You'd kill me even if I told you," Indy said.

"Perhaps, but I would do it quickly instead of

spilling your intestines onto the deck of this flatcar. There are no surgeons on this train, Dr. Jones, and you would bleed to death despite the best efforts of your friends to patch you up."

"And why wouldn't you kill Wu Han if I told you?"

"His services are too valuable to Lao Che," the voice said. "He wants him back. To waste a good employee in such a profitless manner would show poor business sense. But your pathetic expedition is another matter. It would delight the boss to see it end before it even begins."

"Who the hell are you?" Indy asked.

"A professional."

"Like your buddy? Or was he just having a bad day?"

"He was careless. I am not."

Granger was at the door of the passenger car, a 7.5mm bolt-action rifle in his hand. Indy waved and smiled, and motioned for him to go back. Granger looked confused, and stepped over onto the first flatcar.

"Tell the old fool to get back into the car."

"He can't hear me," Indy said.

"Then shoot him."

Indy felt blood roll down between his shoulder blades as the knife pressed harder into the soft hollow at the base of his skull.

"*Kill* him."

Indy pointed the Webley at Granger and shot. The bullet thudded into a crate behind him. Granger looked aghast, not knowing whether to laugh or to return fire.

"Idiot!" he cried.

Indy rolled forward, exposing the assassin. Granger snatched up his rifle, but the dark figure had scrambled down behind the cargo before he could manage to get off a shot.

Indy crawled back to the flatcar, where Granger was kneeling behind one of the trucks and trying to get a clear shot at their opponent.

"Are you all right?" Granger asked.

"That's a relative question," Indy snapped. "Look at the back of my neck."

"It's nothing," Granger said.

"Nothing? It feels like I'm bleeding to death."

"Flesh wounds always flow like the dickens." Granger's tone was dismissive. "Who is that chap, anyway?"

"An associate of your gangster friend, Lao Che."

"No friend of mine." Granger sniffed. "But one uses what is at hand to get the job done, you know. Jones, did you really have to take a shot at me?"

"He was holding a knife on me," Indy said. "Besides, I missed on purpose. I'll bet you're glad the train didn't hit a bump just then, huh?"

"I don't know where you got the idea that you could shoot." Granger shook his head. "Concentrate, Jones, squeeze the trigger gently. I've watched you, and every time you shoot you hold your breath and snap the trigger like a four-year-old kid with a cap gun."

"Sorry to interrupt your little chat," Joan said as she crawled up next to them, "but what do you intend doing about that fellow in black? If you haven't noticed, he's slicing open the canvas over the truck up there."

"I told you to keep her back," Indy scolded.

"I can't argue with a nun," Wu Han said.

"What the devil is he up to?" Granger asked.

"Say, that big machine gun mounted on the truck isn't loaded, is it? I mean, you didn't fit it with a magazine yet, right?"

"It wouldn't be of any use if it weren't."

"Terrific," Indy said.

"Oh, I doubt whether the bugger will be able to figure out how to operate the thing. It's rather complicated, you know, and most of these simple people have no experience with advanced firearms. If it's not a muzzle loader, they're lost."

The assassin brought back the bolt on the British machine gun and chambered a round. He was crouching in the back of the truck, and the muzzle of the gun was pointed into the air. He test-fired at the sky, laughed maniacally, then swung the barrel down and let go with a short burst at the truck where the others were hidden.

The front end of the Dodge truck quivered as

bullets chewed into it, shredding the canvas and sending bits of metal and glass spraying upward. When the shooting stopped, the truck settled down on two flat front tires and began to hemorrhage oil and antifreeze.

"I think we ought to be hunting for a safer place to hide," Granger suggested. "This particular flatcar is loaded with petrol drums."

"Indy," Wu Han said. "What's the plan?"

"I don't have a plan," Indy replied. "Why do I always have to be the one with a plan?"

"You just do," Joan said. "So make one."

"Jeesh." Indy took off his hat and jammed it onto Joan's head. "Take care of this for me. I don't want any holes in it, you understand?"

"What do you want me to do?" Granger asked.

"Keep him pinned down in the truck," Indy said.

Indy sprinted to the forward end of the car and jumped down onto the coupling while .30-caliber slugs riddled the area where he had been. His boots slipped on the grease-covered iron, but he caught himself before he fell.

He took hold of the frame of the flatcar and began to pull himself along beneath it. As the roadbed whizzed beneath him Indy imagined the killer trying to point the machine gun at the deck. If there was a way to do it, he decided, the assassin would probably figure it out.

Finally Indy reached the end of the flatcar and

grasped the tongue with both hands. The heels of his boots sparked on the roadbed as he pulled himself up onto the coupling. Then he crouched on top of the coupling, resting briefly between the cars. He studied the mechanism for a moment, then drew his pocketknife and jammed it deeply into the brake hose. He had to twist with all of his might, but finally the blade punctured the tough hose with a hiss of escaping air pressure. Then Indy pulled the pin and strained against the lever that opened the coupling. Finally, it turned.

"Let's see how you deal with *that*," Indy announced.

As the cars began to separate, Indy realized he was on the wrong side of the coupling. As the gap widened between the cars he would become a sitting duck for the assassin's machine gun, and there wouldn't be enough time to scramble to safety, regardless of whether he was on the top, side, or bottom of the car.

The cars were now held together only by the damaged hose. As the drag of the rear cars increased, the line was drawn like a bowstring. Indy leaped to the tongue of the forward car just as the brake line snapped at the wound he had made earlier.

Suddenly free of part of its burden, the old locomotive picked up speed. Ahead, the tracks gradually dipped downward in a slow curve to a river valley.

The rails crossed high over the river on a wooden trestle.

Indy waved sheepishly at his friends on the retreating car. Then he drew the Webley and climbed cautiously up onto the deck of the flatcar, making sure to stay low enough behind the cargo so that the assassin couldn't see him.

With the help of the gradually decreasing grade, and no sign of a brake, the locomotive was gaining even more speed. As the train fanned out around the curve Indy made his way to the side of the flatcar and waved his arms to try to get the attention of the crew up in the locomotive. Smoke and sparks belched from the stack. Surely they knew if they didn't slow the train down, they were going to jump the tracks and plunge into the river at the bottom of the curve.

Indy stopped waving.

The windows in the cab of the locomotive were empty, even though the pair of drivers on each side of the engine were churning furiously against the rails. The crew had left the throttle open and jumped into the nearest irrigation ditch when the shooting started.

"This is no way to run a railroad," he said.

Indy peeked over the top of a crate. The assassin was still in the back of the Dodge, both hands on the machine gun, searching for a target.

"Cut us loose!" Indy pleaded.

His answer was a burst that riddled the top of the crate.

"Look, you trigger-happy polyglot," Indy shouted. "We're both going to die if we don't do something quick. I'm coming over the top of this crate, so don't shoot."

Indy holstered his gun. He held his hands in the air, fingers spread. He squinted, clenched his teeth, and eased himself up. When he was fully erect and found that he had not been shot dead, he smiled and placed his hands on his hips.

"Good," he said. "I knew I could talk a little—"

The assassin was frantically working with his knife to clear the breech of the gun. The gun had jammed during the last burst, and a shell casing was stuck sideways in the ejector, preventing it from firing.

Indy jumped up onto the hood of the truck.

"Get away from there," he ordered as he pulled his revolver.

The assassin backed away from the machine gun.

"Now uncouple us. Do it, quick!"

The flatcar was rocking back and forth on its springs as the train rocketed toward the river. The assassin walked cautiously to the front of the car, pulled the pin, and raised the lever. The car did not, however, show any tendency to leave the rest of the train.

Indy put the gun in his belt and grasped the wheel to set the brakes manually. The wheel was stiff with rust.

"Help me," he said.

The assassin got on the other side of the wheel. The wheel began to turn, slowly at first and with the sound of tortured metal, then more quickly. Sparks flew from the wheels of the flatcar. At this speed, the brakes were merely an annoyance to the car's momentum. With agonizing slowness, the locomotive and the rest of the train began to move ahead.

"Good," Indy said.

The flatcar was only twenty yards behind the rest of the train when the locomotive left the tracks and plunged over the side of the trestle to the river below. The tender and a half-dozen freight cars were pulled over the side as well.

Indy ducked.

The locomotive exploded as the cold river water seeped into the superheated boiler. The debris from the blast peppered the trestle and the flatcar like shrapnel.

The rails were badly warped, but unbroken, where the train had left the track. The flatcar bucked fiercely as it clattered over the damaged section, then lost speed and rolled to a smooth stop on the other side of the river.

"We made it," Indy said, struggling to his feet. "Hey buddy, we made it!"

But there was no response from the assassin. He was lying dead on the deck of the flatcar, a boiler bolt protruding from his forehead.

3

WANSHAN PASS

The expedition's three flatcars, pushed by a tiny switch engine, had finally rolled to a stop at track's end in the city of Kalgan. It had taken a hired crew most of the morning to unload them.

"We don't have room for all of the equipment," Wu Han told Indy as the gang pushed the bullet-ridden Dodge down a pair of makeshift ramps. The truck's flattened front wheels refused to follow the path indicated, however, and the workmen scattered as the front end of the truck fell off the ramps. The truck slid the rest of the way on its frame, then bounced as the rear wheels struck the ground.

"We need three trucks, not two. What do we do, boss?"

"Have you ever driven a team before?" Indy asked.

Indy took off his fedora and wiped his forehead with a dusty sleeve. Despite the cold, he was sweating from the morning's work.

"That was nice work back there, Jones," Granger said. "Not only did you manage to destroy a locomotive and most of a freight train, but you ruined exactly one third of the expedition's vehicles and put us two days behind schedule in the process. I can't imagine Brody will be very happy about that, my brown-eyed friend."

"Please," Wu Han said. "It wasn't Indy's fault. The assassins . . . and the machine gun . . ."

"Granger has a very warped sense of humor," Indy told Wu Han. "But don't worry, he's just having some fun at my expense. If he were really angry with me, he wouldn't say a word."

"Oh," Wu Han said. "But that doesn't make sense."

"Nothing has so far on this expedition," Indy concluded.

"What are we going to do about that ruined automobile?" Granger asked. "I don't think we can afford to abandon the rest of our supplies here."

"Do you suppose this town has a blacksmith?"

"Of course," Wu Han said.

"Then find him. See if he can put the truck back into working order. I don't think the block is cracked, so hopefully it will just be a matter of patching the radiator and so forth."

"But Indy," Wu Han protested, "I doubt if this town's blacksmith has ever seen a new American automobile, to say nothing of repairing one."

"We'll have to chance it," Indy said. "Besides, you seem to know a little about everything. And we have to have that third truck, or else we won't have enough supplies with us to return from the middle of the Gobi."

Indy counted out some bills and gave them to Wu Han.

"This is the last of our paper money," he stated. "I spent the rest of it on that sorry excuse for a locomotive to take us the rest of the way. But it should more than take care of fixing up the truck. And make sure you have plenty of petrol when you leave."

"And that's all the money the expedition has left?"

"No," Indy said. "That's just the last of our paper money. The Great Wall is seven miles from here, high up on that mountain, and once we pass through, our paper money is worthless. From that point on, it will be strictly gold or barter."

By the time Wu Han found a blacksmith, ascertained that the modifications could be made, and reported back to Indy, the two running automobiles were loaded with all they could carry.

"The work will take the rest of the day," Wu Han said. "Perhaps more. The blacksmith said that was as fast as he and his apprentice could work."

"But can he fix it?" Indy asked.

"It was a little difficult for me to understand his dialect," Wu Han said, "but he promised me that he could make it *go*. I told him he would have to answer to the white devil who leads our expedition if he failed."

"Granger, of course."

"No, Indy. The white devil is you."

"With each mile we go," Indy said, "it's like we're going back in time. Airplanes, locomotives, and now blacksmiths to fix a twentieth-century horseless carriage. By the time we get to Professor Starbuck, we'll probably be in the Stone Age."

"Why don't you go ahead?" Wu Han suggested. "The weather is mild and there is plenty of daylight. The expedition is far enough behind schedule already."

"Are you sure?" Indy asked.

"Of course."

"Pick the best hired man to stay on with you, at least for a little while, because crossing the wall alone is often the last mistake a traveler makes," Indy said. "Also, always keep your gun handy. Don't be afraid to use it. These people have seen you with the expedition, they know you have money, so be careful."

"But Indy," Wu Han said. "I don't have a gun."

Indy opened one of Granger's crates and picked

up a Colt .45 automatic. He showed Wu Han how to load it, then gave him a box of cartridges.

"Remember," Indy explained, "when you load the clip into the butt for the first time, you have to pull the action back. That puts a round in the chamber and cocks the hammer at the same time. Got it?"

"Yes, boss," Wu Han said.

Indy stuck the Colt into Wu Han's waistband.

"Keep it there, where people can see it." He paused. "And if you have to draw it for any reason, count on shooting it, even if you have to fire a round into the air. It's bad luck and a sign of cowardice to these people if a weapon is drawn and not used."

"I don't like guns, Indy."

"Good," Indy said. "The best kind of person to use one. Now, if all goes well we will make camp about thirty miles on the other side of the wall tonight, along the road to Urga. But if you're not there at first light—assuming the repairs take longer than expected—then we'll have to leave without you. In that case, you catch up with us as best you can."

"Don't worry, Indy. You can count on me. I owe you much more than my life, and we Hans pay our debts."

Indy climbed into the cab of the truck. He stepped on the starter switch and the six-cylinder engine ground for a moment, then sputtered to life.

"Xanadu," Indy said, taking a last look around. "It is said that Kubla Khan built his summer palace a few miles from here. You know, the Coleridge poem..."

" 'In Xanadu did Kubla Khan a stately pleasure dome decree,' " Joan recited. "I'm sorry, but this doesn't look much like paradise to me."

The pair of trucks left the city and struck out on the old road that followed the riverbed up to the Mongolian plateau. Granger was in the lead, driving the truck that had the machine gun mounted on the back. In some places, the wheels of countless carts had cut so deeply into the road that all Indy could see of the truck ahead was the barrel of the machine gun.

Joan was surprised at the number of people on the road, some with carts but many on foot, carrying goods to and from the market at Kalgan.

"Where do you suppose they all come from?" she wondered aloud.

"Look closely at the hillsides," Indy said. "The people here live in dugouts and caves for the most part, because they are warm in winter and cool in the summer. But because the dugouts are the same color as the earth around them, you have to look sharp to see them."

Seven miles outside of Kalgan they reached the foot of the pass, at an altitude of just over three thousand feet above the plain. The road turned abruptly upward, and Indy had to use low gear to keep the truck from stalling on some of the steeper grades.

"This is a pass?" Joan asked.

"This is the flat part," Indy said.

They climbed another two thousand feet in the space of eleven miles, on a road that was filled with switchbacks and doglegs. Indy had to fight the truck to keep the wheels from becoming mired in the deepest of the ruts, or jumping as they bounced over rocks that would qualify in some parts of the world as boulders. Just when Joan thought they would never reach the top, they rounded a corner...and before them stretched the Great Wall of China.

Granger had pulled to the side of the road. He was sitting on the running board of the truck, calmly smoking his pipe and admiring the view.

Indy brought the truck beside Granger's.

"Look where we've been," he said.

Stretching to the south was mile after mile of tortured hills that looked as if they had been torn from a geography classroom's relief map of China. In many places the hills had been cut raw by wind and rain, and the wounds exposed the very backbone of the earth.

"No wonder my rump is sore," Joan said.

Coiling around these broken ridges, like a serpent hoary with age, was the Great Wall—the biggest, and certainly the longest, structure in the history of the world, stretching for nearly four thousand miles over northern China. Some parts of the wall were two thousand years old; but this part, which had been built and rebuilt over the centuries, dated from less than a thousand years past.

The wall was forty feet wide at its granite base, and between the battlements on the top ran a road paved with bricks that had been trod by generations of workers and soldiers. The inside of the wall was filled with earth. And all of the work on its construction had been done by hand, one stone and one cartful of earth at a time.

Indy leaned out of the window of the truck.

"Granger, you drive like a madman."

"I had to," Granger returned, clenching the stem of his pipe between his tobacco-stained teeth. "I was terrified because I knew you were behind me. Are we ready to cross over?"

"I'll take the lead for a while." Indy put the truck into gear and eased it forward.

The road passed beneath the Great Wall through a gate in a fortresslike watchtower that stood four stories high. The gate was open, however, and the watchtower was manned only by crows.

"This was originally built to keep out the Mongol invaders," Indy said as the shadow of the wall engulfed the truck. "It failed, however. Genghis Khan swept over the wall like the god some said he was, and conquered most of China."

"So what good was it?" Joan asked.

"Quite a lot, actually," Indy said, blinking against the darkness. "Its real value proved to be as a magnificent make-work project that pulled China together as a nation, much as the pyramids did in Egypt."

"We could use some of that at home right now," Joan said.

A figure darted in front of them and shouted something.

Indy did not understand the command, since it was delivered in a dialect he had never heard before, but the intent of the rifle-toting figure who had planted his feet in front of the truck on the Mongolian side of the gate was plain enough: his right arm was extended with his palm toward them.

Indy stood on the brakes and the wheels skidded to a stop. Granger, who was following close behind, was not so quick on the brakes. Although they were only going a few miles an hour, the front bumper of his truck smacked Indy's hard enough to shove it forward a few feet.

The raked grille of the Dodge had barely touched the greasy pants of the soldier, but he jumped as if the truck had bitten him. His dark eyes burned with disgust. He muttered something about demons in motorcars, then, with the barrel of his fifty-year-old single-shot rifle, motioned Indy out of the truck.

Indy slid slowly from behind the wheel, his hands in the air.

"I take it you're not from the Mongolian Traveler's Aid Society?" Indy asked. "Or has living out here made you so stir-crazy that you just throw yourself in front of moving vehicles as a form of amusement?"

The soldier hissed.

"Apparently you don't understand English," Indy said.

The soldier drew a greasy piece of paper from a leather pouch he wore around his neck. He unfolded it, smoothed it out, and handed it to Indy.

"Can you read it?" Joan asked.

"Yes." Indy took his glasses from his shirt pocket. "Chinese writing is pictographic, which means it is based on pictures. It isn't phonetic. That's why he carries it, I think, considering the number of dialects that must pass through this gate. This is smudged, but I think I can make it out. What is this spot here. Blood?"

"Stop teaching school, Jones," Granger called. "Just read the damn thing."

"It says his name is Feng, and that he's an envoy of the great General Tzi. Feng is to be treated with the respect deserving his position, blah blah blah, member of the Rotary and the Cutthroat Chamber of Commerce. Just kidding. Anyway, Tzi has appointed him as gatekeeper of the south, and all travelers must present themselves for the inspection and approval of Feng before proceeding or they risk incurring the wrath of Tzi himself."

Indy handed back the paper. Feng held the rifle in the crook of his arm while he tucked it safely back in the pouch, then returned the pouch beneath his shirt.

"Okay, here we are for your inspection," Indy said. "I hope we meet your approval. I'm Jones, and this is Sister Joan, and that one behind us is called Granger."

Feng snapped his fingers impatiently.

"I think he wants papers," Joan suggested.

"What's the trouble?" Granger called from behind.

"Stay in your truck, Walter," Indy said pleasantly as he pulled his passport and visa from his jacket pocket and handed it to the soldier. "Don't shoot, not just yet."

Feng opened the passport, flipped quickly through the pages, then tossed it back at Indy, who caught it in his still-raised left hand.

"I don't think he can read," Indy said.

"Then what could he want?" Joan asked.

"Money, what else?"

Indy gave Feng his most winning smile and reached slowly for his revolver. He picked it up by the ring on the end of the grip and placed it on the hood of the truck. Then he pointed to the soldier's gun and made a downward motion with his hand.

The soldier hesitated, then lowered the gun.

Indy smiled again and reached inside his shirt.

The gun came back up.

"Wait," Indy said. "Let me show you what I have."

Indy took a single gold piece from the pocket of the money belt and held it up. It was an American eagle—a ten-dollar gold piece—and it was a little less than the size of a quarter, but much heavier. Feng grinned, took it, and bit into the edge of it with jagged teeth.

"Why do they do that?" Joan asked.

"Real gold is soft," Indy said. "If they can bite into it and leave a mark, they know they've got the real McCoy."

Feng squatted, but kept his rifle upright between his legs. He placed the coin on the ground and motioned for Indy to join him in a palaver.

"He wants to talk," Joan said.

"He wants to negotiate. He figures there's more where that came from."

Feng pointed at the coin, then pointed at Indy's truck, and with his finger made five marks on the ground. Then he pointed at Granger's truck and made five more marks.

"Ten," Indy said. "He wants ten gold pieces to let us pass."

"The man is obviously deranged," Granger said. "Ten dollars is more money than most of these nomads see in a decade, and one hundred is out of the question. I've never heard of this General Tzi. He probably wrote up that little paper himself in order to squeeze some dishonest money out of people like us."

"Keep your shirt on," Indy called. "We're not done yet."

Indy shook his head at Feng. He smoothed over the lines Feng had made, pointed to both trucks, and made one mark on the ground.

Feng hissed and rubbed out Indy's offer.

He drew seven marks on the ground.

It was Indy's turn to hiss.

Feng held his hand up in a conciliatory gesture. He erased the last two marks, then pointed at Joan through the windshield of the truck and grinned wickedly.

"I think we may have a deal," Indy said.

"Don't even think about it," Joan spat.

"Okay, okay," Indy conceded.

Indy held up two fingers, then pointed at Joan and shook his head gravely.

Feng held up four fingers.

"No," Indy said. Then he took two more eagles, placed them on the ground beside the first one, and folded his arms. He took a step back on his haunches, to emphasize that it was his final offer.

Feng tapped his fingers on his rifle butt. He looked at Indy, then at the trucks, then back down at the coins. Finally he scooped up the gold pieces, wrapped them in a dirty rag, and shoved them deep into his pants pocket.

"Done," Indy said. "Thirty dollars."

"It's still robbery," Granger muttered.

The trucks emerged from the gate onto the Mongolian plateau.

Feng slunk back to his lean-to against the wall, put his rifle down, and sat next to the cook fire he had abandoned when he heard the sound of the trucks. A rodent was roasting on a spit over the flames.

A dog chained to the wall paced and watched with hungry, intelligent eyes. Instead of a collar, the end of the log chain was looped tightly around the dog's neck and fastened with a padlock.

Indy stopped the truck.

There was something about the dog. It was a purebred Alsatian, Indy judged from its deep chest and head, a breed of shepherd noted for their intelligence and loyalty. This Alsatian was male, and it had blue eyes. It was missing its right ear. The wound had healed, but it bore other signs of abuse; not only was it starving, as attested to by the painfully thin stomach and protruding ribs, but its back carried a lattice of whip marks.

Feng tore off a piece of the rodent and popped it into his mouth, chewing contentedly. The dog walked forward until all the slack was out of the log chain, then began to whine for a piece of meat.

Feng told it to shut up.

The dog bared its teeth and snarled. Indy had never seen such hatred in the eyes of an animal. It fought against the chain like a wild thing, biting and chewing the links, attempting to free itself.

Feng muttered and went to retrieve a horsewhip that hung from a peg inside the lean-to. Then, careful not to cross into the radius described by the log chain, he began to whip the dog furiously. Instead of yelping, the dog snarled and attempted with each blow to catch the whip in its mouth.

Feng cried out in surprise as the end of Indy's bullwhip bit into his wrist. He did not know that Indy had left the truck at the sound of the first blow, and that Indy's whip was bigger and longer than the one he was using to beat the dog.

"How do you like it?" Indy asked.

Feng dropped the horsewhip.

"It *hurts,* doesn't it?" Indy asked.

Feng made for the safety of the lean-to, with Indy's bullwhip popping and snapping over his back as he ran. He grabbed his rifle and turned to shoot, but he discovered that Granger was standing behind Indy with his repeating rifle ready for action.

Feng dropped his gun.

"You can tell General Tzi," Granger said, "to go to hell."

Indy took up the spit with the rodent carcass and strode toward the dog. The dog growled, its one good ear going low against its head and the hair on its back bristling.

"I'd be careful if I were you," Granger said. "That animal looks as if he could tear a man apart, and considering what Feng here has done to him, it would be justifiable homicide. It would be better to put the dog down, considering the sorry shape he's in."

"We're not going to kill this dog," Indy said as he dropped to his knees. He held out the carcass, and the dog quickly lunged for it and tore it from the stick. Then it began choking down great chunks of meat and bone.

"Sister Joan," Indy called. "Bring me the bolt cutters from the toolbox in the truck bed."

Indy reached out to pet the dog.

The dog snapped viciously at him.

"I don't want your food," Indy said soothingly. "Just come here. I'm trying to help you."

Joan brought Indy the long-handled tool, and while the dog finished the carcass Indy slipped the jaws of the cutter beneath the chain at the dog's neck. Then he strained to bring the handles together, and with a *chink!* the dog was free.

"I think we'd all better get back in the trucks," Granger said, backing away while holding the rifle on Feng. "I think I'm more frightened of the dog than I am of this character here."

"Why was the dog chained to the wall like that?" Joan asked as Indy got into the truck. "Is it some kind of barbaric custom?"

"No custom that I know of, Sister."

As Indy started the truck Feng began to rant while standing just outside the door of his lean-to. He swore vengeance on Indy, on Indy's children, and his grandchildren. He vowed to make Indy pay for showing disrespect to an envoy of General Tzi, and he hoped desperately that Indy understood him.

Then Feng spat and threw the gold pieces in the dust.

Indy popped the clutch. The trucks sped away.

The dog, suddenly aware that it was free, trotted beyond the perimeter of the chain. Then it made a run for Feng, who dashed inside the lean-to and slammed the door in the dog's face. Then he sat cross-legged inside the shack, his rifle across his lap, shaking from fear and anger.

After an hour of waiting, the dog looked longingly toward the north, where the trucks had disappeared. Then he glanced at the setting sun.

The dog trotted off toward the north.

When Feng was sure the dog was gone, he came out of the shack and dug the gold coins out of the dirt.

4

DESOLATION ROAD

"It's time to go."

Indy nodded, but lifted the binoculars and searched the horizon one last time. They had spent the night without incident in the gently rolling Tabool Hills, and in the bone-chilling cold that came before dawn Indy had climbed a ridge overlooking the Urga Road. On top of the ridge was an *obo*, a conical pile of stones that travelers had left in appreciation for safe journeys thus far.

The sun was now well above the horizon.

"Have you seen anything?"

"Just that dog," Indy said.

"The one from the wall?" Granger asked.

"The dog has apparently been following us," Indy said. "He stays on the horizon, close enough not to lose sight of us, but not within rifle range."

"Damn," Granger said.

"You're not going to shoot him."

"If he comes prowling into camp, I will," Granger vowed. "An animal that has been mistreated as badly as that one is liable to do anything. It could rip your throat out before you even knew what hit you."

"It had a chance to rip mine out and didn't."

"You were lucky," Granger said.

"I hope Wu Han's lucky, too."

"I'm sure he's fine. He is a resourceful chap, you know. It's my guess the blacksmith couldn't finish the job in one day. Don't worry. Wu Han will be along in time."

"I hope you're right," Indy said. "Between Kalgan and Urga are three hundred miles of the worst road on earth, and that's not counting parasites like Feng. Do you have a stone?"

"What?" Granger asked. "You don't expect me to believe in such foolish superstitions, do you?"

"Come on," Indy insisted. "Fork it over. I know you better than that, and we can use all the help we can get, whether we believe in it or not."

Granger removed a fist-sized rock from the pocket of his shooting jacket. Indy took it and placed it squarely at the apex of the curious monument.

At noon the next day the little motorcade pulled into Tuerin, the halfway point on the road to Urga.

Nothing moved in the little windswept hamlet as the trucks made their way to the center of a knot of buildings.

Indy cut the ignition and sat for a moment, listening to the silence broken only by the incessant wind. A dust devil swept down the main street, scattering trash and old newspapers, then disappeared as quickly as it had formed.

"Is this a ghost town?" Joan asked.

"No," Indy said. "We're being watched, you can count on that."

Granger got out of his truck and pulled his rifle out behind him. He slung it over his shoulder and then went to the front of his truck, where he unhooked a canvas bag of water that had hung from the bumper. He knocked the dust from the bag, uncapped it, and took a long drink. Then he wet his bandanna and wiped his face and neck.

Indy walked over to Granger and stared at the ground. Then he crouched and picked up a corroded brass shell casing. Similar casings were scattered everywhere.

"Four thousand Chinese soldiers were massacred here twelve years ago," Granger said. "The army was annihilated by a force of three hundred mounted Mongols, under the direction of a Russian baron. The Mongols rode for days to get here and then struck at daylight, after resting their ponies for only a few minutes. In the end they saved their ammunition and clubbed the Chinese to death with the butts of their rifles or ran them through with sabers. The few Chinese who escaped into the desert froze to death. It was forty degrees below zero."

"The shadow of Genghis Khan," Indy muttered, and dropped the casing.

Indy took the canvas water bag and handed it to Joan before taking a drink himself. Joan's face was caked with dust and her habit was smeared with mud. The trucks had become mired in a mud hole when the road crossed a narrow stream forty miles back, and it had taken all of them to free the wheels.

"Are we camping here tonight?" Joan asked.

"Yes," Indy said. "This is where we buy our camels. We need to set up the mess tent over there, in that little clearing, and we will put this on top of the highest pole to announce our presence."

From his pouch Indy took a strip of blue silk and handed it to Joan. It was a foot wide and three feet long.

"It's a *hata*," Indy said. "Sort of like a Mongol calling card."

In twenty minutes they had the tents pitched and Granger was preparing lunch over a gasoline camp stove in the mess. Lured by the aroma of coffee and sizzling pork, the inhabitants of Tuerin, with their children in tow, had slowly emerged from their homes to inspect the visitors.

Granger placed the food in the center of the wooden table while Indy poured three mugs of steaming coffee.

"I hope you made enough for everybody," Joan observed.

"Don't be preposterous," Granger scoffed. "We can't feed the entire village. We have to make this food last."

"The children look hungry," she said.

"Do you think they would feed us if the situation was reversed?" Granger asked.

"Yes," Joan said calmly, "I think they would."

Indy placed the pot back on the stove and looked out the open door of the tent to the crowd that had gathered. Most were women and small children, although there were a few old men. They stood a few yards beyond the mess, their hands folded diffidently in front of them.

"Where are the men?" Joan asked.

"Two thirds of the male population of Mongolia are lamas," Granger said, getting up. "I could never understand their religion, although I have asked plenty of them about it. Supposedly a special sect of Buddhism, under the rule of the Dalai Lama—the living god, as they call him—but I think it's a rather elaborate con game. A rather cushy life, if you ask me, holed up in their monasteries. I guess they can pray better with their bellies full."

Granger closed the tent flaps.

"And the other third of the male population?" Joan inquired.

"Bandits, of course."

Indy regarded his plate of meat and vegetables and took up his fork. He stabbed a piece of canned pork and held it to his lips, then threw the utensil down.

"Granger, I can't eat when those people are hungry."

"Neither can I," Joan said.

"Missionaries." Granger looked disgusted. "All right, we have quite a few boxes of powdered milk and more canned pork than I suppose we absolutely need. We can go back to the old system of hunting for our supper when times get rough, I suppose. But I warn you, Jones, we may be eating rodent before this is over."

"Better to eat a rat than to be one," Indy concluded as he rose to find the powdered milk.

"Can't I even eat my lunch first?" Granger complained.

Joan tied open the flaps. Then she stepped outside and, taking the hands of one somber-eyed little boy and his mother, led them inside and seated them at the table. She took Granger's plate and placed it in front of them.

"No," Joan said. "You can't. Guests first."

The rest of the crowd followed.

For the next hour Indy and Joan were busy preparing food and placing it before the apparently inexhaustible appetites of the people of Tuerin. When the last plate had been wiped clean, an elaborately robed figure filled the doorway of the mess tent.

The man stood at least six feet tall and had a long black mustache that drooped over his pronounced chin. In the crook of his arm was a Russian-made rifle. His black eyes glanced from face to face.

Silently, the women gathered their children and left. Only one old man was left at the table with the American adventurers, and he was busily gumming the last of his pork.

"Who feeds my children?" the man asked in English.

"Who would not?" Indy asked.

The man broke into a laugh and strode into the tent.

"You Americans," he said, gesturing expansively at the surroundings. "Every day is like holiday for you. But I am grateful for your hospitality, even though it should be us that are feeding you."

Indy held out his hand and they shook hands.

"I am Indiana Jones," he said, then introduced Granger and Joan.

"I am Meryn," the man said with a flourish. "My

friends will tell you that I am the best camel driver in all of Mongolia. Others will agree that I am the best and quickest thief. And my enemies—ah, if only they could speak from the grave!—they would tell you that I am the fiercest warrior."

"I hope we're going to be friends," Indy ventured.

"Of course we are friends," Meryn roared. "An enemy does not feed your children, even after he takes your wife. But you can have your pick of my wives. I see you have already met three of them."

"Which ones were they?" Joan asked.

"Why, the most beautiful, of course."

"We are in need of a good camel driver," Indy said.

"Then you have found him. Tell me, are you friends of the great Andrews? My father drove camels into the heart of the Gobi for Andrews many years ago, when the Americans discovered the hiding place of the fossils of the great *allergorhai-horhai*. He told me before he died that he would have followed Andrews to the gates of hell itself."

"I knew your father," Granger said. "I am sorry to hear that he is dead."

"The Chinese," Meryn said sadly. "Or the Russians. Then again, it could have been the Japanese, I am not sure. We never found the body. But I am comforted by the certain knowledge that he took many of the dogs with him."

"I'm sure he did," Indy said.

"You speak English very well," Granger observed.

"My father," Meryn explained.

Granger poured a mug of coffee and placed it on the table. Meryn slung his rifle from a tent pole and sat down. "How many camels will you need?"

"Many," Indy said.

"What I don't have I will steal for you," Meryn said, sipping the coffee. "Do you have sugar?"

"Steal?" Joan asked as she placed a tin of sugar before him.

"Just a figure of speech." As he spoke Meryn spooned so much sugar into the mug that the coffee threatened to overflow the rim. Then Meryn pressed his lips to the cup and began to slurp down the syrupy concoction.

"Tell me, have you ever heard of a chap by the name of General Tzi?" Granger asked.

Meryn nearly choked on the coffee.

"Tzi!" he spat. "Where did you learn of the detestable name?"

"We ran into an envoy of his at the Great Wall on this side of Kalgan, a rather unpleasant fellow by the name of Feng," Granger said.

"I hope you killed him."

"Unfortunately, no."

"Tzi the Cannibal," Meryn continued, "calls himself a general and claims that he is a patriot in the fight against the Communists, but he spills the blood of all. He sends his troops out from an impregnable mountain fortress, where he lives under the protection of the False Lama of the Black Gobi."

"What's the False Lama?" Joan asked.

"The lama equivalent of the Antichrist," Indy said.

"The False Lama is the rival of the Living God at Urga," Meryn explained. "In the confusion since the Communists have outlawed the religion, the False Lama managed to attract a small band of followers and marched into the desert. Tzi would be nothing if not for the evil power of the Black One."

"That's comforting," Indy said. "Why do they call him the cannibal?"

"Because he is rumored to eat the hearts of his victims," Meryn said. "He is relentless and tracks his prey using a pack of wild dogs that he feeds human flesh."

Joan blanched. "That's . . . hard to believe."

"I'm afraid not," Granger said. "Wild dogs are particularly dangerous in this country because many of them develop a taste for human flesh. That's why I was so concerned with the beast Indy freed at the wall. And don't think I haven't noticed, Jones, how you have been leaving food outside the camp for that killer."

"How do they develop this appetite?" Joan wanted to know.

"In the smaller villages, superstition is rampant," Granger said. "Dead bodies are considered so unclean and such a breeding place for evil spirits that when a person dies, they throw them onto the back of a cart. Then the village's bravest man takes off with the cart, going hell-bent for leather across the countryside and never looking back. Eventually the body is bumped off the cart, where it becomes food for the dogs."

"That's the stuff of nightmares," Joan declared.

Granger sighed. "If only it were just bad dreams."

"Now, let's talk of more pleasant things," Meryn suggested. "What kind of price will you pay for these camels you so desperately desire?"

Joan was exhausted but, in the lonely silence of her tent, found that she could get no rest. Every time she closed her eyes, her mind conjured up visions of wild dogs with glowing eyes that trailed her relentlessly across the desert.

Finally, she gave up. She dressed, put on a heavy wool overcoat, and stepped outside the tent. The wind had stopped and the stars were shining. She walked and leaned against Indy's truck, thinking about her father.

A dog began to bark.

Joan froze. The barking was coming from some-where in the darkness, and it was growing louder. She drew her coat around her and took a few steps toward the tents.

The dog that Indy had freed from the wall came bounding into the middle of the camp, baying like a mad thing. It planted itself between Joan and the tents, its legs spread, the hair on its back bris-tling.

"Don't move," Granger told Joan.

Granger had slipped out of his tent and held his rifle in his hands. He clicked off the safety, then slowly brought the rifle up to his shoulder.

"Oh my God," Joan said.

Joan was in the line of fire. Granger began stepping slowly to the side, in an attempt to get a shot at the animal without risking Joan in the process.

The dog advanced, still barking wildly.

"I'm almost there," Granger said. "Remain still."

"Oh my God," Joan repeated.

Granger took two more steps to the right and be-gan to squeeze the trigger gently. The dog broke into a run. Indy knocked the muzzle of the gun into the air just as Granger fired, and the bullet went zipping into the night sky.

Joan crumpled to the ground as the dog leaped.

The animal sailed over her and landed squarely on the chest of Feng, who had been creeping up on the nun with his knife drawn. Feng fell backward and the dog sank its teeth deeply into his wrist.

Other figures raced into the camp now, wielding knives and guns, and Granger chambered another round and shot the closest of them in the chest. The brigand fell with a sickening sigh at Indy's feet, a dagger still clasped in his lifeless hand.

Indy drew his revolver and charged the attackers, firing as he went. They scattered, but not before one of them managed to slice open Indy's cheek with a saber.

"Not again," Indy moaned, stanching the blood with the palm of his hand. "It just healed."

Feng kicked himself free of the dog and ran into the night, throwing curses behind him.

"Not very brave, are they?" Granger mused.

"It doesn't take much courage to kill people while they sleep," Indy said. "Sister, are you all right?"

"Just shaken," she said. "If the dog hadn't . . ."

"Don't even think about it," Indy said. He knelt and patted the ground. The dog cautiously walked up and allowed him to place a hand on his head. "If Loki here hadn't started barking like he did, we'd probably all be dead."

"I'm glad I was wrong about the animal," Granger said.

"I had a dog when I was a kid and I never got over it when he died. He was my best friend."

Then Indy added so quietly that the others couldn't hear, "My namesake, as a matter of fact."

"You've named him Loki?" Joan asked.

"Sure," Indy said. "For the Norse god of mischief who was chained to a wall."

5

CITY OF THE LIVING GOD

At gunpoint, a pair of policemen walked Indiana
Jones and Walter Granger out of the dank prison
where they had spent their first night within the ancient walled city of Urga. Neither had slept, and
they had been subjected to repeated interrogations
in Russian about their presence in Mongolia.

Standing flat-footed on the street, Indy blinked
into the sunlight. His nose itched fiercely, but, like
Granger, his hands remained tied behind his back.

"Aren't you going to untie us?" Indy asked.

One of the policemen shoved the barrel of his gun
into the small of Indy's back and pushed him forward.

"I'd take that as a no," Granger said.

Both of the guards were Buriats, members of a
northern Mongol tribe that had for generations

considered themselves Russian. Neither spoke as they forced Indy and Granger through the crowded streets, nor did they smile when Indy joked—in Russian— about how grateful he was for the free accommodations for the night and the excellent food.

"Where do you find roaches of that size?" Indy inquired.

The city stretched for five miles along the Tola River, and despite the best efforts of the Communists, it still retained its character, a curious mixture of three cultures—Chinese, Mongolian, and Russian. The Russian buildings were invariably squat, utilitarian structures painted in red or orange, while the homes resembled ornate cottages; the traditional Mongol buildings had great palisades of rough-hewn wood around them atop which fluttered prayer flags; and in the city's business district there was row after row of prim Chinese shops with their wooden counters and blue-jacketed merchants. What had been removed from the architectural scene since the Communists had come to power in 1924, however, was any sign of a religious life. The city's churches, chapels, and monasteries had all been leveled. Taking their place were sandbagged machine-gun nests; these ugly structures dominated every important intersection.

The Russian consulate was a huge red building that stood on the site of a Catholic church that had been demolished shortly after the Communist takeover. Although the Mongol government was supposedly autonomous, nothing happened without the approval of the Russian officials.

Indy and Granger were forced up the steps, down a corridor of bleak stones, and were shown to a stark office where Joan was already waiting.

"Are you all right?" Indy asked.

"Yes," she said.

"Is this a trial?" Indy asked in Russian.

"Of course not," the foreign minister said from behind his massive desk. He was a small, balding man with a bad complexion, and his name was Badmonjohni. He pressed his fingertips together as he leaned over his massive desk toward them.

"Then why are we under arrest?" Indy asked.

"You are not," the minister replied. "You were detained for twenty-four hours under suspicion of espionage, but after questioning Sister Joan here, I am confident that you are harmless, if misguided."

The man motioned for the Buriats to leave.

"Where's my dog?" Indy wanted to know.

"He is downstairs, locked in a cage that is ordinarily used for leopards," the minister said. "He is quite unhurt. I'm sorry I can't say the same for the policeman who wrestled him out of the cab of your truck and put a leash on him. It took a number of stitches to repair the damage, and in the end they had to lasso the animal like in one of your Wild West shows. But then, I've been told that Urga reminds you Americans of your western frontier days."

Indy smiled.

"What about our trucks?" Granger asked.

"They are outside, waiting for you," the minister said pleasantly. "We even filled the tanks with petrol and checked the oil for you."

"Service with a smile," Indy quipped. "Look, we were on our way to this office when your thugs jumped us and dragged us off to prison. Our intent was to obtain the proper credentials for the remainder of our journey."

"We are sorry to have caused you any discomfort," Badmonjohni said. "I hope you will accept my sincerest apologies. But such things are difficult to arrange, Dr. Jones. Ordinarily such permits take months to process, and that is in the most peaceable of times. We weren't expecting a trio of Americans to burst into the city with an armed motorcade and demand safe passage across the Gobi."

"But surely some consideration can be made for a mission of mercy," Indy began haltingly. It had been some years since he had spoken conversational Russian, and he found himself searching for the right words. "I'm sorry, but my Russian is rather awkward. May we please speak English?"

"Of course."

"We are here to find Professor Starbuck and return him safely to his family."

"The good sister has explained all of this to me, and I am not unsympathetic to your mission," the minister said. "But the region is unstable. The Russians distrust the Chinese, the Chinese distrust the Russians, and everyone hates the Japanese. There will be rumors of espionage and intrigue."

"Look, we're not spies," Indy declared. "This is a scientific expedition funded by the Museum of Natural History. We have two objectives—first, to locate Professor Starbuck, and second, to return intact whatever fossils he may have found. It is that simple."

"As a practical matter, there is very little difference between a scientific expedition and a strategic one," Badmonjohni said. "Both are out to collect information, photographs, maps. We have not let an expedition into the Gobi for several years for that very reason. You have wireless and photographic equipment with you, no?"

"You know we do." Indy was growing impatient. "Our trucks were searched."

"That will be a very difficult thing to get around," Badmonjohni said. "But if you would agree to make certain concessions, perhaps a deal could be arranged. It would take several weeks to iron out the details, however."

"We don't have weeks," Joan said. "In another month it's going to be forty below out there on the desert, and my father could freeze to death before we find him."

"There could be a way to speed things up,"

Badmonjohni suggested. "But it won't be easy. What I am trying to say, Dr. Jones, is that it will not be cheap."

"Ah, now we get down to business," Indy said.

"This one apparently decided not to go into religion," Joan observed.

"How much?" Indy asked.

"How can you expect me to bandy about figures when we're talking about such a difficult thing?" Badmonjohni returned. "It is insulting."

Indy turned his back to the minister, reaching inside his shirt, and took a handful of gold pieces from his money belt. Then he turned and placed them on the desk.

"Perhaps this will soothe your pride."

Badmonjohni swept the gold pieces into a desk drawer without counting them.

"I will try, Dr. Jones," he said. "Come back in three days. We will know then whether my efforts have been successful or not. In the meantime I suggest that you and Sister Joan do some sightseeing, in the event the request is denied. Then, perhaps, your long journey to Mongolia might not be considered wasted. By the way, I suggest for your own sake that you stop referring to the city as Urga. That city is dead. This is Ulan Bator, the Red City."

"Thank you," Indy said grudgingly.

"Oh, Dr. Jones," Badmonjohni added. "We have taken the liberty of keeping the shortwave, the cameras, and that curious machine gun until your request is decided. Each of the other guns you carry will require a ten-dollar permit, and the trucks will be fifty. You may pay those fees now if you'd like."

"How much did you give that Buriat thief?" Granger asked when they were outside.

"About five hundred dollars," Indy said as he and Loki descended the steps of the consulate. "I expect it will take another five hundred to complete the deal."

"Bloody Reds," Granger said.

"What do we do now?" Joan asked.

"We sightsee," Indy said, "and make ourselves as inconspicuous as possible for the next few days."

"It is too bad that religion has been outlawed," Joan commented. "I would have liked to have visited the Dalai Lama."

"Well, you still can," Granger said. "Religion may be illegal, but it's sort of like Prohibition was in the States—that doesn't mean that you can't get it. You just have to know where to find it. The Dalai Lama has moved underground, and he resides in a compound on the outskirts of town surrounded by a dozen fawning monks. Of course, the last duly recognized Dalai Lama died in 1923, and there is some dissent over whether this one is truly the most recent incarnation of Buddha on earth, but I'll take you to meet him. It's not every day you get a chance to meet God Himself, is it, Sister?"

Inside a compound surrounded by a palisade of rough-hewn poles, in a little yellow cottage with a green roof, they were ushered into the presence of the Living God by a pair of monks in flowing red robes with sky-blue cuffs.

Indy stood stiffly at attention with his fedora in his hands while Granger slouched behind them with his hands in his pockets. Indy bowed, pulling Joan down with him, while under his breath he told Granger to show a little respect.

"My word," Granger said as he doffed his hat and bowed.

"We're pleased to meet you," Joan stammered.

The Lama was a middle-aged man with milky-blue eyes and a shaven head. He sat on a pillow cross-legged and he wore a simple saffron robe over black trousers.

"Come closer," the Lama said. "My eyes are failing me. The doctors say I will be completely blind by spring."

"I'm sorry," Joan said as they moved forward. The monks in the red robes brought a trio of pillows. Indy told Granger to tuck in his feet as they sat down.

"Don't be, my dear," the Lama said. "I have seen

enough of the suffering of this world, while the beauty of it will never fade from my mind's eye. I have seen you coming for several weeks now, and such a long journey you have made! Across the sea and over the land."

"You have seen us?" Joan asked.

"In my dreams," the Lama said. "I have also seen packs of wild dogs, and bandits, and much hardship ahead."

"What else can you tell us?" Joan said.

"What can one tell from dreams?" the Lama asked. "That you are on a journey not of the body but of the soul is obvious, my dear. You are seeking that which has been lost for a very long time."

"My father," she said.

"More than your father," the Lama said. "You search for the ancient of ancients, the world as it was before it was corrupted by knowledge. The Garden of Eden."

"Yes, you are right," Joan said quickly. Then: "Will I find it?"

"Who am I to say?" he asked. "It is up to you. I only see into my own dreams, not into your heart."

"Excuse me," Indy said as he pulled a scrap of orange cloth from his shirt pocket, "but are you sure that your spies didn't tell you we were coming? Surely you sent the monks after us in New York."

The Lama inspected the scrap of cloth.

"It means nothing to me," the Lama said. "You act as if perhaps it should. But this particular piece of cloth is from one of our remote monasteries, deep in the Gobi."

"You can tell that just by looking?" Granger asked.

"No, by touch," the Lama replied. "The weave is unmistakable. Tell me more about these monks that you say were after you. What did they want?"

"They took the horn," Indy said.

"Ah, a horn." The Lama sighed. "Now we are getting somewhere. Can you describe this horn for me? No, wait. Let me show you something and you tell me if it resembles the thing that was taken from you."

He spoke to the monks, and presently one of them brought him a brightly colored reliquary. The Lama said a prayer, then opened the top of the wooden box and removed a horn that was a smaller version of the one that had been taken at the Museum of Natural History.

"Does this look familiar?" he asked.

"Yes," Indy said, inspecting the horn. "But it is not the same one that was taken from us. This is smaller. It's also fossilized."

"It has been handed down from generation to generation and is unimaginably old," the Lama said, replacing it in the box. "Do you know what it is?"

"Do you?" Indy asked.

"Of course," the Lama said. "It is the horn of the fabled *allergorhai-horhai,* the sacred stone beast of the desert. Many say the *horhai* is just a myth, but here we have a bit of tangible evidence, a reminder of the unfathomable cycles of the world. You are familiar with this beast?"

Indy said that he was.

"It is said that it still lives in the Gobi."

"I have heard as much."

"Is the beast the object of your search?"

"We are here to find Professor Angus Starbuck, who is lost somewhere in the Gobi. Sister Joan here is Starbuck's daughter."

"But you also seek the beast. Otherwise you would not have shown me this scrap of cloth," the Lama said. "I have heard of your Professor Starbuck. He is well-known in the monasteries across the desert, and I will help you in your search for him if I can. As I recall, he was last seen in the region of Gurbun Saikhan."

"I know the place," Granger said quickly. "It is near what is called the Flaming Cliffs, where the Andrews expedition found many excellent fossils."

"Gurbun Saikhan," Indy repeated. "The Three Good Ones."

"It was named for you three ages ago," the Lama stated.

Granger snorted.

"Preposterous," he said. "Probably some poor nomad shot three antelope at the spot."

"Perhaps it would be helpful if you replaced your hat on top of your head," the Lama suggested. "Your hearing—or at least your listening—seems to be somewhat impaired."

Indy laughed.

"Do you know anything else of my father?" Joan asked.

The Lama shook his head. "He is rather a mysterious figure, and whatever he finds during the long treks in the desert he keeps to himself.

"Dr. Jones," the Lama continued. "I wish you the best in your attempt to locate Professor Starbuck. But there is something I must now ask of you."

"I will do whatever I can," Indy said.

"If you should happen to find the *horhai* in your search for Professor Starbuck, you must agree to keep it safe from harm. Can you do that?"

Indy paused.

"The *horhai* is a mythical beast," he said.

"The most important truths are often found in myth."

"But what would you have me do to protect it?"

"The answer to that is in your soul," the Lama said. "When the time comes, you will have to search honestly inside yourself for the answer. That is often the most difficult thing for a man of action to do. Can you do that, Dr. Jones?"

"Yes," Indy replied.

"Good news," Badmonjohni said as the trio filed into the foreign office at the Russian consulate. "I have worked day and night and have finally obtained the necessary permits for your expedition."

"Excellent," Granger said.

Badmonjohni placed the papers on the desktop. Included was each of their passports, and they had been stamped with the appropriate visas.

"There are just one or two minor details," the minister said. "You must, of course, surrender all of your photographic and wireless equipment. The machine gun is out of the question, of course. And I must have seven hundred more dollars."

"What?" Granger said. "Are you trying to wipe us out?"

"Goodwill must be spread around in order to produce the desired result." Badmonjohni shrugged. "The amount is not negotiable."

Indy counted out the gold and piled it on the desk as Granger swept up the permits.

"There is one last requirement," the minister said. "Absolutely nothing can leave the country without first being inspected and approved by the People's

Republic of Mongolia. All of your specimens must be brought back here to Ulan Bator for examination."

Granger looked at Indy.

"No problem," Indy said. "We'll have to come back this way to pick up Sister Joan anyway."

"You can't expect to leave me here in this godforsaken place," Joan pleaded as they left the consulate. "Where am I going to stay? In the women's prison?"

"Well, you *are* familiar with it," Granger observed.

"The Lama has taken a liking to you," Indy said. "He has invited you to stay at a cottage on his compound until we return, and I suggest you take him up on the offer. It is the safest place for you here."

"I won't," she said.

"Look, Sister," Indy said. "We had a deal, remember? You were to go as far as Urga, and that was all."

"You had a deal," she stammered. "I didn't say a damn thing. You just assumed that I agreed to it."

"The cursing nun," Granger said. "How proud your order must be of you."

"You can go straight to—"

"I get the idea," Granger interrupted. "Now listen to me. Are we going to have to tie you up and deliver you to the compound, or are you going to act sensibly for once? I swear, I'll tell the monks that you're crazy and that you have to be locked in your room for your own good if I have to."

Joan was silent.

"We're doing you a favor," Granger continued. "Do you want to meet those wild dogs for real instead of just in your nightmares?"

"All right," Joan agreed. "You can take me to the compound. But you'd better leave me enough money to take care of myself until you get back."

As soon as the trucks pulled out of sight of the compound, Joan gathered up her things and set out on foot for Urga's business district, the reassuring weight of ten gold pieces swinging in the pocket of her habit.

6

WILD DOGS

With two automobiles and thirty camels strung out in a long line over the sculpted dunes, the expedition at last penetrated the Gobi.

Granger's truck, minus the machine gun, was in the lead. An American flag fluttered over the cab, attached by a long staff to the bed of the truck. Although the sight of the Stars and Stripes always caused a patriotic murmur in Indy's heart, the flag was there for a practical reason as well: so the truck could be easily located as it dipped below the dunes while Granger scouted the best route for the caravan.

Indy's truck flew a blue pennant emblazoned with the logo of the American Museum of Natural History—the skeleton of a man attempting to control the skeleton of a rearing horse. The inspiration for the design came from one of the museum's most popular exhibits, but Indy liked the piratical quality of the thing—in the remote Gobi, where the Mongols revered horses and were frightened of the dead, it spoke unintended volumes.

The going was slow, and Granger constantly checked their progress against his compass and his maps. When they stopped for the evening he would use his sextant and astronomical schedules to fix their exact position, then determine the altitude with a barometer and make a note of it in his log. The maps that were available of the area were as devoid of detail as maps of the open sea.

Occasionally the desert would yield to hardpan covered with stunted trees that resembled tamarisk, but they passed no watering holes. Animal life was scarce and human habitation was nonexistent; in the week since they had left Urga, they had not met another human being—except for frequent sightings of a Buriat soldier on horseback who had been dispatched by the foreign minister to spy on the expedition. When the soldier's horse died of exhaustion, they invited the incredulous man to join the expedition but told him he would have to do his share of the work for food and water rations. The grateful soldier quickly agreed.

Sometimes they would encounter a bleached skeleton sitting next to a weathered food bowl, near the telltale circle of stones where a Mongol yurt—a squat conical-shaped tent—had once stood. The Mongol practice was to pull up stakes and abandon those who were dead or dying to unmerciful nature. Although Granger found it shocking, Indy could see the stark necessity of the practice; the Plains Indians of North America were known to have done something similar during hard winters.

During the days it was hot enough that Indy was forced to shed his leather jacket, but at nights the temperature plunged to freezing or below. Meryn and the other drivers seemed to accept these extremes without hardship, but Indy found that the cycle sapped his strength. He was used to harsh conditions, but usually for only a day or two, and then it was back to base camp for a hot shower. Out here, there was no water to spare.

Granger, however, was finally in his element. He hummed over morning coffee and made detailed notes in his log by the light of a Coleman lantern until well into the night.

His mood deteriorated on the morning of the seventh day when Joan suddenly rode into camp on a piebald horse that was worked into a dangerous lather. She had abandoned her habit for a purple Chinese tunic, jeans, and boots, and on her hip was an old-fashioned single-action revolver. A flop hat was tied to her head with a rag. Her lips were parched and she was badly sunburned.

"Surprised to see me?" she croaked.

Then she fell from the saddle into Indy's arms, and the horse promptly collapsed and died.

"What were you thinking?" Indy asked as he soaked a rag in water from the canteen and placed it on Joan's forehead. He had placed her in his tent so she would be out of the sun. "Didn't you believe us when we told you how unforgiving the desert is?"

"I believed you," she croaked, "but I also believed I could catch up with you in just a day or two. Something inside me was telling me that I had to be on this journey, that you couldn't find my father without me. I didn't intend to kill that horse, honestly I didn't."

"You're lucky he made it all the way, Sister," Indy said. "If he had given up the ghost just a few hundred yards earlier, we would never have found you."

"How is she?" Granger asked through the tent flap.

"Baked, but not done. Frozen, but not spoiled. She'll live."

"Good," Granger replied. "Pardon me, Jones, but could I have a word with you out here?"

"You rest," Indy told Joan. "I'm leaving the canteen here, but don't drink too much water at one time or you'll cramp up. Okay?"

"Thanks." Joan paused. "And . . . I'm sorry."

"I'm just glad you're alive," Indy said. "You must have one helluva lucky star up there."

He left the tent with Loki trotting behind. He

joined Granger, who was standing far enough away so that Joan couldn't overhear. His hands were behind his back and he was puffing furiously on his pipe.

"Can she travel?" he asked.

"Tomorrow, maybe," Indy said, scratching Loki's head. "But I'm afraid we're stuck here for at least a day."

"Blast that woman," Granger sputtered. "I thought nuns were supposed to act, well, like *nuns*. They're supposed to stay put when you tell them to."

"Like a well-trained horse?"

"You know what I mean," Granger snapped. "She has endangered the entire expedition. The drivers are predicting disaster because of the presence of a foreign woman, and I can't say I blame them. We have to maintain a certain speed as we cross this wasteland. We are forty miles from the nearest well, and there is no guarantee that it won't be dry."

"Maybe we should leave her behind with a little bowl of food."

Granger was silent.

"I'm beginning to come around to her view of things," Indy said. "Anybody who is that desperate to find her father deserves to come along on the search. If she were a man we wouldn't think twice about it, would we?"

"Yes, but she's not a man. That's exactly the point."

"What, because she's a woman she can't possibly endure the privations we'll face? Do you know what she did when she ran out of water back there, Walter? She drank her own sweat. Said she read an article in *National Geographic* about the bedouins doing it. How many men do you think would have the presence of mind to do *that*?"

Granger lapsed again into silence.

"Let's talk to Meryn," Indy suggested. "Have him explain the situation to the drivers. Tell them that she's a holy woman—which isn't a lie, now, is it?—and that we need her to find Professor Starbuck. Tell them to make camp, we'll be staying here for a day or two. And tell them if they don't like it, they can march off in any direction they please."

On the morning of the second day the journey resumed, with Joan riding in the truck with Indy. None of the camel drivers had left, but Granger continued to sulk. Meryn had complimented Joan on her courage, and made an extravagant ceremony out of presenting her with a good-luck tassel made from the claw of a leopard to wear from her belt. In return, she gave him her rosary beads.

"*Sai!*" Meryn had exclaimed, and held his thumb in the air to show his approval before tacking the rosary to the butt of his rifle.

"Does that mean you've given up your vows?" Indy asked.

Joan did not answer.

They reached the well in the afternoon.

It wasn't much of a well by Western standards, just a pile of rocks around a lopsided hole, but the tracks of men and animals surrounding the little oasis attested to its importance. Indy dropped a bucket over the side and was relieved when he heard a splash as it hit water.

"Thank the gods," Granger breathed. "Now, we must be careful with our use of water. This well is fed by a little underground spring that seeps, instead of flows, so we must be careful not to exhaust it. If we do, we may be sentencing the next poor devil that comes this way to death by dehydration."

Granger prescribed the order in which things would be done: the animals would be watered first, then the drivers could drink and fill their water bags, then the radiators of the trucks were to be topped off. Only then would Granger allow Indy to erect a makeshift shower stall from a couple of squares of canvas and a rope stretched between the beds of the trucks. He declared a strict ration for each bather— there would be a common bucket of water to soap with, and one full bucket for each individual to rinse. The Mongols, of course, thought this entire ritual was insane.

Indy was the last of the trio to shower, and he

used his water sparingly. He brushed his teeth and shaved first, then lathered up and poured the bucket of water slowly over his head and body. When he was done he felt better than he had in weeks.

"That was wonderful," he said to no one in particular as he emerged from behind the canvas, cinching on his gun belt. It was a warm afternoon, and he had left his shirt unbuttoned in order to feel the breeze on his skin.

"No kidding," Joan said.

Indy jumped.

She was sitting on the bed of the truck, brushing her long brown hair. A towel was wrapped tightly around her torso, but her arms and legs were bare, and despite the towel's attempt at modesty, it made her figure even more pronounced. Indy paused to speak to her, but was suddenly bereft of words.

The others were far on the other side of the truck.

"What's the matter?" she asked.

"I'm sorry," Indy stammered. "I just noticed how good you smell."

Joan appeared unfazed by this remark. "We all do after a bath."

"No," Indy said. He glanced over and noticed how her bare feet dangled above the ground. "I mean, it's different."

"Dr. Jones." Joan's lips were tight. "Are you looking at my legs?"

"Sorry," he said. "They're nice legs."

"You're just sorry you got caught," she teased. "Have you been in the desert so long that you've resorted to flirting with a nun? At least, I think I still am. I'm not sure. It's been increasingly easy to forget."

"No kidding," he said.

"What I mean is, there's nobody to care what you do out here. It's just the wind and the sky and the desert. Nobody's breathing down your neck trying to tell you how to live or how to get closer to God. Know what I mean?"

"Look, I need to get some work done," Indy said. "I've got lots of things to do that I'd better get right on top of—"

"It's the difference between religion and spirituality, I think," she said. "Religion is an institution. Its business is to perpetuate itself by telling people what to do. But spirituality is an individual's own personal relationship with the Almighty."

"Do you want your clothes? I'll get your clothes for you if you want them," he offered.

"I can get them," she said.

Joan slid down from the bed of the truck, and as she did, the towel she was wearing gathered and rose above her knees. Indy glanced quickly away, and his head was still turned as she walked over and placed her arms around his neck.

"You know what, Dr. Jones?" she whispered in

his ear. "I don't think God wants me to be a nun anymore."

Indy swallowed.

"And you know what else?"

"No," he said with a rasp. "What?"

"I think I've succeeded in scaring the daylights out of you." She flicked his earlobe with her finger. "Shame on you for looking at me like I was the blue-plate special. And shame on me for enjoying it."

A moment later Meryn bellowed the alarm.

"Bandits!"

The fast-moving Mongol ponies swept toward the well like the wind, and Indy barely had time to pull Joan down with him beneath the bed of the truck and draw his Webley before the bandits were upon them. The poor Buriat soldier that had been sent to track the expedition on horseback was the first to die, a lance driven through his neck.

Meryn shot the lead bandit out of the saddle with his single-shot rifle, then lunged at the next while swinging the rifle like a club. The butt hit the bandit in the stomach, knocking him from his horse. When he hit the ground Meryn was on top of him with a curved knife, and he slit his throat in one motion.

Then Meryn himself fell as a slug took him in the shoulder.

"You stay here," Indy told Joan.

Indy dashed from beneath the cover of the truck and into the thick of the battle. A bandit rode between him and Meryn and Indy gripped the horse's bit and twisted fiercely, causing the iron to gouge the soft palate of the horse's mouth. The animal fell over in a blur of teeth and flashing hooves, pinning its screaming rider beneath.

Indy reached Meryn, grasped his jacket collar with one hand, and began to pull him toward the safety of the trucks while keeping up a regular barrage with the Webley. They had almost made it when a particularly ferocious-looking bandit on a prancing black pony cut them off.

Indy pointed the Webley at the bandit's head and pulled the trigger. The hammer fell with an impotent click on a spent cartridge.

"Time out?" Indy said hopefully.

The bandit shouldered his musket and the muzzle hovered over Indy's chest. Then there was the thunderous report of a large-caliber rifle ... and the bandit's blood rolled down onto the front of his shirt.

On top of the bed of the truck, Granger worked the bolt on his 7.5mm rifle and a cartridge flew from the breech. Then, with workmanlike precision, he drove home a fresh round and took aim at another target.

Indy pulled Meryn beneath the truck. Loki was there, with Joan, and he was growling.

"How're we doing?" he shouted to Granger.

"We're losing," Granger said between shots. "There must be thirty of them, and we're down to six. And they've made off with half of our camels."

"Where's your gun, Sister?" Indy asked as he reloaded the Webley.

"Up on the bed of the truck, with my clothes."

Indy stood up, firing as he went, and snatched down the holstered gun.

"You had better start using it if you want to stay alive," he said as he tossed it at her. "If you hadn't noticed, things are serious."

Joan pointed the revolver at the whirling blur of one of the bandits and fired, but nothing happened. Then she shot twice more, and the bandit went down.

"Good," Indy said. "Keep it up."

Suddenly the camp became quiet, but there was so much smoke that Indy could not tell what was happening. Granger jumped down from the bed of the truck and crouched next to Indy.

"What do you make of it, Jones?"

"I don't know," Indy said.

"Perhaps they withdrew."

"I don't think so." Indy shook his head. "They had us where they wanted us. Wait—do you hear that?"

"My God," Granger breathed. "It's the baying of dogs."

"They've brought the dog pack in to finish us

off," Indy said. "Quick, we need to get into the cabs of the trucks. It sounds like there are a hundred of them, and we can't shoot them all."

The bandits drove the dogs into camp and the animals surged around whatever was on the ground, including the fallen bandit comrades, and began to shred flesh from bone.

Joan buried her face against Indy's shoulder.

"I can't watch," she said.

Then the dogs discovered the survivors beneath the bed of the truck. Loki vaulted into the pack, and a terrific fight ensued, while Indy and Granger emptied their weapons at the closest animals. Driven by the scent of blood, the dogs were briefly distracted as they fell upon their own wounded.

"Keep shooting," he told Joan. "This is worse than serious."

The dogs were coming from all sides now, snapping at hands and faces and tearing away bits of clothing. Indy and Granger placed Joan between them and continued to fight.

One of the dogs sank his teeth into the heel of Meryn's boot and began to drag the unconscious man from beneath the truck. Granger shot the animal and hauled Meryn back, suffering a number of bites on his own hands and arms as he did so.

"This is a helluva way to die," Granger remarked.

The volley of a dozen rifles shook the camp,

followed by a second and then a third volley. The dogs began to scatter, leaving many of the pack behind to die, and then the bandits retreated through the camp, pausing only to fire a shot now and then at whatever was advancing toward them.

In a few moments the camp was still once again, although it now stank of nitrate and was littered with the bodies of men and dogs. Through the blanket of gun smoke that floated at shin level, Indy could see a pair of Mongol riding boots striding toward them.

"The dogs have gone."

Indy and Granger crawled out.

The stranger was tall, elegantly robed, and carried an ornate matchlock rifle in the crook of his arm. On his belt was a knife whose silver handle was studded with gems. He held the reins of a magnificent white horse, an Arabian, and behind him loitered a dozen men like himself.

"We are grateful," Granger said.

"Don't be," the stranger said. "I am leaving you with your lives, but it looks as if Tzi's men have made a shambles of your caravan. It may have been more merciful to let you die quickly now rather than later, and much more slowly, in the desert."

"Thanks for giving us the choice," Indy said.

"I will require something in exchange for my services, since my men do not ride for free. A few camels, perhaps, ammunition. We could work something out if the woman is for sale."

Indy looked down at Joan. She was propped up on her elbows beneath the truck, dressing Meryn's shoulder, and the towel threatened to fall away from her upper body. Suddenly aware of the eyes on her, Joan pulled the towel back up.

"She's mine," Indy said quickly.

"Too bad," the man said. "I have been eager to make the beast with two backs with a Western woman, but I have not yet found one that is willing. Why do you suppose that is? Here in Mongolia, women consider it an honor to share themselves with guests."

"It is our custom," Indy said, "that we do not."

"What a backward race you Americans are."

"I say, are you chaps bandits as well?" Granger asked.

"It is an ugly word," the Mongolian said. "We prefer corsairs, privateers, pirates, raiders, guerrillas, irregulars, mercenaries, or simply, patriots. We steal so that we can continue our fight against the Communists."

"We have a little money we would gladly share with you." Granger held out a fistful of coins.

"Bah!" the man said, and struck the coins to the ground. "What do we care for money out here on the desert! Where would we spend it, what would it bring us? Give us food, water, grain for our ponies, women for our pleasure, and guns and ammunition so that we may slay our enemies. These are the things that make up the life of a man. Do not insult us with the bits of trash you grovel after in the cities."

"Who are you?" Granger asked.

"I am Tzen Khan, a descendant of the great Genghis Khan, and this is my band. We live free or die. We do not ordinarily come to the aid of foreign caravans, but I admire courage above all things. You fought well and sent many of the human dogs to the netherworld where they belong."

Khan stepped forward and peered intently at Indy's face.

"I like you," he said. "I do not know why, but I like you. We have met before, I'm sure, in some other lifetime long ago. I can tell by the fire behind your eyes that you have always been an adventurer, an interloper in strange lands. Who knows? Among the thousand names we have worn, perhaps you were Marco Polo and I, Kubla Khan!"

"Perhaps," Indy said.

"Come to my yurt and we will discuss the battle in detail. My camp is just over those dunes, not more than half a kilometer. It will be cold tonight, and your injured friend should be protected from the elements. And do not fear because I have plenty of goat!"

"Indy," Joan said. "What do we do about the dead?"

"We follow the Mongol custom," he said, "and let the desert take care of them."

Indy spent twenty minutes, however, searching for Loki among the dead. The injured dogs he encountered he shot; not for vengeance, but for mercy.

With the exception of Meryn, all of the camel drivers were dead. So were a score of fallen bandits that were scattered about camp; Khan's men had made sure of that, and had used their knives in order to conserve ammunition.

Indy found no sign, however, of Loki.

Khan's yurt was an eighteen-foot conical tent of layered felt that stretched over a lattice frame of willow branches, which, despite its solid appearance, could be erected or taken down in less than half an hour. Joan was amazed when she parted the felt door to see that inside, the yurt was as well-appointed as any Western living room.

There were bright rugs and lavishly carved furniture, including an imposing red lacquer chest that had a picture of the Buddha on it. The walls were hung with quilts. The rope bed doubled as a sofa, and in one corner there was an iron stove with a stack that led up through the roof of the tent. On top of the stove was a large iron pot of slowly cooking onions and goat.

"Why don't we travel with these?" Joan asked.

"Because we're stupid Westerners," Indy replied as he and Granger helped Meryn inside. "We sleep in those freezing, thin-walled tents that just about any stiff breeze can knock down, then we congratulate ourselves on being civilized."

They placed Meryn on the rope bed. Indy opened the medical kit, and as he proceeded to change the dressing and sprinkle sulfa powder on the wound, a woman and a young girl dished out plentiful helpings of the goat stew. The girl was about seventeen, with luxurious black hair, and neither of them spoke while they worked.

"Is it serious?" Joan asked.

"No," Indy said. "The bullet passed through. He will heal, in time, as long as we can keep it clean."

When Khan's daughter placed a wooden bowl of stew beside him, Indy noticed that her face was scarred, as if from a terrible case of acne, only worse.

"What is wrong with your daughter?" Joan asked.

"She is not my daughter," Khan said. "I rescued her and the woman from one of General Tzi's bands. They both would have been sold into slavery if I had not found them. They stay here now of their own will, and they are free to go if they wish."

"Tell us about this Tzi," Granger said. "Those were his troops that attacked us, were they not?"

"Of course," Khan concurred. "No one but Tzi uses wild dogs. His citadel is not far from here, perhaps three or four days. I will visit him someday, when the power of the False Lama is broken, and I will rub him out."

"Getting rid of the competition?" Granger asked. "I mean, he is a rival of yours."

"More than that." Khan's eyes filled with hatred as he spoke. "Tzi murdered my family. My wife, my three beautiful children. Princesses all. He was jealous of their affection for me, so he ate their hearts."

"Literally, he ate their hearts?" Granger asked.

"I understand that he cooked them first."

"How horrible," Joan said.

"I was driven mad with despair and wandered the desert for days until my best friend found me and brought me home to my yurt. Later, when Tzi discovered that I held another living thing dear to me, he kidnapped my best friend. He tortured him to death, then sent me his ear as a reminder."

Joan shuddered. "How horrible."

"Quite," Granger said, rubbing the stub of his own mauled ear.

"That is why I am no longer close to anyone," Khan went on. "That is why the woman and the child do not speak to me. Even though they sleep here in my yurt, I live alone."

"Khan," Indy said. "If you have vowed not to make friends with anyone for fear of endangering their life, then why did you tell me you liked me?"

Khan's answer was nonchalant. "Oh, I did not think you would survive long anyway."

"Terrific," Indy said.

"Khan," Joan asked, "what's wrong with the girl's face?"

"Smallpox," Indy answered. "She was lucky to have survived."

"He is right," Khan said. "Many of my band have suffered with this disease. Those it does not kill, it marks, like her. Once you have it, though, it never comes back."

"We have medicine for that," Indy said. "Vaccines. Shots. It would spare those of your people who have not had the disease from getting it. We all have had it, so we do not fear catching the disease. But we could share the smallpox vaccination with you, and show you how to use it, and give you other medicines that will fight infection. Many of your people will live who otherwise would have died."

"This is good," Khan said. "I have known of such remedies for some time, but never dreamed they would be brought to the very door of my yurt. This would make us stronger, in order to fight the

Communists. And to kill Tzi, when he is no longer protected by evil."

Khan slapped Indy on the back.

"This is what I will do. In exchange for the medicine, I will reprovision your caravan and provide an escort to the edge of my territory, which is three days' ride from here. But beyond that I can do nothing, because the land is under the control of Tzi and the False Lama. If the spell were broken, I could do more, but I dare not. Bullets are no match for black magic, and I must bide my time until I can avenge the deaths of my wife, my daughters, and my best friend."

"I wish you the best of luck," Indy said.

"And I, you!" Khan smiled. "It has been pleasant to have a friend again, if only for a little while. I hope that we meet in your next life as well, but perhaps it would be more interesting to be enemies, no? If only I had an enemy I could admire, then I could die a happy man."

"Stick around," Granger said. "The Communists may prove to be more than a match."

One week and a dozen minor adventures after leaving the protection of Khan's band of brigands, the caravan—with the two automobiles and ten camels driven by Meryn—reached the base of the Flaming Cliffs. An imposing and gigantic structure of red sandstone, the cliffs rose from the desert plateau like a page from a child's storybook—brilliantly hued, and resembling nothing so much as impossibly gigantic fortresses, cathedrals, and spires.

Within two minutes of bringing the trucks to a stop, Granger had uncovered the first broken shells of dinosaur egg and showed them to Indy.

"This place is lousy with them," Granger said. "You can't walk a hundred feet in any direction without stumbling over them. When we first found them, we thought they were birds' eggs—imagine, just ten years ago, we didn't even know how dinosaurs reproduced."

Indy took the bit of shell and rubbed his thumb across the porous surface. It felt just like a chicken's egg, only larger.

"Maybe dinosaurs were just a type of big bird," he suggested.

"You need to work on your humor, Jones," Granger observed. "It's getting a little stale."

"Sorry," Indy said.

"Why are there so many fossils here?" Joan asked. "I mean, they have found fossils elsewhere in the world—Montana, for example, and even Kansas—but nothing to compare with what has been found around these red sandstone cliffs."

"Nobody knows for sure," Granger explained, "although much of it may have to do with the unchanging nature of this particular corner of the world. It apparently looks just as it did sixty to eighty million years ago, during the late Cretaceous, the last hurrah of the dinosaurs."

"I feel like I've stepped back in time," Joan said.

"Imagine what wonders some of those cliffs must contain," Granger said. "There are hundreds of square miles to explore here, and we have barely scratched the surface in the handful of expeditions that have come here during the last ten years."

"Has anyone actually climbed up into those cliffs?"

"Not far," Granger said. "They are too rugged."

"But they're so beautiful. Like the Grand Canyon, the Petrified Forest, and Pike's Peak all rolled into one."

"Meryn!" Granger called. "We'll set up camp here. Secure the animals and then establish the mess and a latrine. I imagine we will be here a fortnight, at least."

"I can't believe we are finally here," Joan said. "It seems so remote—like we're on the bottom of the ocean or the dark side of the moon. I wish they'd let us keep the shortwave, at least. Or a camera! How I would love to have some photographs of this place."

"Can you draw?" Indy asked.

"A little."

"Then maybe you should start a sketching in the

little notebook you carry and scribble in when you don't think the rest of us are looking. What is that, your diary?"

"I've kept it since I was a kid," Joan admitted. "Well, how do we begin to search for my father?"

"We start knocking on doors," Indy said. "Gurbun Saikhan is just a few kilometers distant, and we stop at every yurt we see between here and there and ask."

Gurbun Saikhan was a mound surrounded by a loose-knit collection of yurts and goat pens. The elder of the village, a toothless man who smoked an old clay pipe, came out to meet them. There was the usual meal of goat stew and token gifts—Indy had hastily picked up a supply of postcards in New York for just such an occasion—and the old man proudly placed a portrait of the Statue of Liberty next to the yurt's portrait of Buddha, assuming the huge torch-carrying maiden was the visiting Americans' preferred goddess.

Although Indy could not understand the dialect spoken in the village, he had brought with him a chalk tablet on which he scratched a succession of Chinese characters to get his point across: *Where did old white man go?*

Luckily the old man was partially literate. He took the tablet and carefully wrote his reply, as if he were taking a test in school:

He went into the sky.

Indy and Joan looked at each other.

Indy could not remember the ideograph for aircraft, so instead he threw out his arms and made an engine noise. Then he looked expectantly at the old man.

"*Bahai,*" the old man said, and shook his head. That much, Indy could understand.

Indy drew a flurry of new characters. *How did he go in sky?*

He walked, of course.

Walked into mountains?

Yes.

Alone?

Yes.

Why?

Didn't ask.

Indy struggled with the next question.

Where in mountains did he go?

Don't know.

That was all they could get out of the old man.

As they prepared to leave, Indy spied a curious piece of jewelry hanging from the wall of the tent. It was apparently a necklace, made of a fragment of carved dinosaur eggshell on a leather thong, and it looked very old. What caught Indy's attention was that the scene depicted in the carving showed a man riding atop a triceratops.

Indy took up his tablet again.

Did you make this?

No. The Old Ones made it. I found it.
Where?
At the base of the cliffs.
May I have it?
Of course. I'll find another—they're everywhere.

"What do you make of this?" Indy asked Joan as they got in the truck. She took the necklace and studied the engraving.

"So the villagers made it," she said.

"They have no idea what a dinosaur is supposed to look like," Indy said. "And this is exactly correct."

"So it's old, it's a fossil."

"You don't understand," Indy said. "It couldn't be. The dinosaurs were all dead before man appeared on earth."

That evening, after supper, Granger examined the piece of eggshell with his magnifying glass. He puffed on his pipe, varied the distance of the shell from the lens, then turned it over.

"Well," Indy asked, "what do you think?"

"I don't know," Granger said. "It is possible that there was a Stone Age cult that lived here many thousands of years ago and worshiped the dinosaur eggs. That much was suggested from the many pieces of jewelry we found made from eggshell and the remains of various cliff dwellings we found on the first expeditions. But this carving is an anachronism; it's impossible, according to what is known of natural history."

"It seems we don't know everything," Indy said. "What if it isn't an anachronism; suppose there was not only a Stone Age culture that revered fossilized eggs, but also living dinosaurs. If there was one spot on earth where a dinosaur might have a chance of surviving into immediate prehistory—and perhaps into twentieth century—it's here. This place *is* the late Cretaceous."

"Jones"—Granger rubbed his eyes—"what a long, strange trip this has been."

"You said it yourself, not twelve hours ago," Indy said. "Who knows what wonders remain to be discovered up in those hills? That's why Starbuck went up into the cliffs, Walter, because *that's* where the trail leads."

At that moment the flap of the tent burst open.

"Meryn!" Granger bellowed. "Don't disturb us. Can't you see—"

Meryn couldn't hear him. His body fell face forward into the mess tent, a wicked-looking knife sticking from his back.

General Tzi's lieutenant, a short young man with a face that was badly marked by smallpox, strode into the tent behind the barrel of a Thompson submachine gun with a fifty-round drum clip. A half-dozen soldiers surged in behind him and began to tie their hands behind their backs.

"What do we do?" Joan asked.

"Nothing," Indy said. "At least not yet."

*   *   *

Indy awoke from the beating the soldiers had dealt to find himself and the others chained to a wall in a cold sandstone cavern. His Webley and his bullwhip were gone, of course, and so was his fedora.

"Are you all right, chap?" Granger asked.

"I think so," Indy said. "At least I can't feel that anything is broken—just bent."

"I thought we had lost you for a moment."

Their wrists were manacled to the wall above their heads, and the cavern was lit by an animal-fat lamp that sputtered and popped and hung by a single heavy chain from the center of the cavern's ceiling. Joan hung between them, her eyes shut.

"How is she?" Indy asked.

"Unharmed physically, I think," Granger said. "But rather in a state of shock mentally. It was the sight of Tzi's soldiers disemboweling some poor herdsmen that put her over the edge. She began to scream hysterically until the soldiers slapped her quiet, then she closed her eyes and hasn't opened them since. It's been close to six hours now, if my sense of time hasn't left me."

"Did you get a chance to peek beneath your blindfold to see where they were taking us?"

"No," Granger said. "But we must be close to the cliffs, with as much climbing as we did."

"What kind of dungeon is this?"

"I'm afraid it's no dungeon. This is where they do most of their meat processing, judging by the bloody pile of bones in the corner. . . . Ah, Jones?"

"Yes, Walter."

"What's the plan?"

"Sorry, I'm fresh out."

There was the rattle of a key being turned in a lock and then the heavy wood door of the cavern swung open. General Tzi, flanked by two of his machine-gun-toting soldiers, waddled into the room.

Tzi was grotesquely fat, with a black Fu Manchu mustache that hung over his jowls and quivered when he spoke. He was wearing a faded green army uniform from the Great War with rows of medals hanging from the chest. The medals were from a half-dozen nations and had been taken from a variety of soldiers he had killed. On the shoulders of the uniform he had pinned large gold stars. Beneath his arm he carried a riding crop.

Perched on the top of his head was Indy's fedora. It was several sizes too small, and the effect would have been comical if Indy had not known who Tzi was.

One of the guards carried a bucket of water, and at Tzi's command he tossed the water into Joan's face.

"Hello," Tzi said.

"Go to hell," Joan sputtered.

"My dear, we are already there," Tzi said. "The Citadel of the False Lama. I have followed your trek across Mongolia for some time, ever since that business with Feng at the Great Wall."

"You must have some communication network," Indy said.

"The False Lama sees everything," Tzi averred.

"Baloney," Granger spat.

"Actually, you are right. Foreigners have marveled for generations over how quickly news travels here, where there are no telegraph lines or radio stations. The answer is quite simple, actually. Gossip travels from well to well like wildfire, and all of my envoys are trained to listen for any information that might be useful to me. Information is power, don't you agree?"

"I wouldn't agree if you said two plus two is four," Indy declared.

"Such courage in the face of certain doom." Tzi's eyes twinkled evilly. "I will enjoy cooking your heart in a little sherry and eating it for my dinner tonight. That also is power, is it not? To consume the organ that is the source of courage? Hmm, you are a university professor, are you not, Dr. Jones? I might just scoop your brains out of your skull as well."

"I hope I give you indigestion," he said.

"Tzi," Granger put in. "I have had quite a career as a big-game hunter and my courage and resourcefulness are well documented. Why, some might even say they are legendary. Why don't you feast on my carcass, old man, and let the others go?"

"You are an old fool whom I find unappetizing," Tzi said. "You, I will feed to my dogs."

"Really," Granger said. "Jones can't even shoot."

"Now, what will I do with this one?" Tzi asked as he placed his riding crop beneath Joan's chin and turned her head to the torchlight. Then he reached out and caressed the front of her tunic.

Joan spat in his face.

"What shall I do indeed," he continued, wiping away the saliva. "It would be a shame to eat you because then you would be all gone! No, I think I shall keep you around a few days to amuse me, then I will sell you into slavery. Many men in this territory are curious about Western women and I will have no trouble finding a buyer. What a profitable venture your expedition has become for me. What a price this one will bring!"

"Tzi..." Joan assumed a businesslike tone.

"Yes, my little concubine?"

"It is apparent that you desire power and knowledge above all things," she went on.

"What a perceptive woman."

"If you get rid of us, you will never know the secret of the *allergorhai-horhai*," she concluded.

"The sacred beast?"

"The same."

"Legend has it that to eat the flesh of the sacred stone beast makes one indestructible," Tzi said wistfully. "But it is just a silly folk legend."

"It's not a legend," Joan said. "We have come in search of the *horhai,* and we were close to finding its hiding place when your men seized us."

Tzi barked orders for the guards to release her.

Joan put her arms around Tzi's neck.

"You know what else the flesh of the *horhai* makes you?" she whispered. *"Immortal."*

"Let us go upstairs and discuss this with the Black One," Tzi said. "He will know how to interpret it. Guards! Prepare these two Americans for the evening meal. Do be careful not to spoil the heart tissue this time, will you?"

The guards slung their machine guns on their backs and advanced toward Indy and Granger with skinning knives. Between them was the water bucket, where they intended to fling the choicest cuts.

"Tzi," Joan wheedled.

"Yes, my morsel?"

One of the guards ran his blade down the front of Indy's shirt, popping the buttons. The second guard, who had hesitated because of the reprimand he had received from Tzi, asked the first guard for advice on technique.

"We need them. They have all the maps and clues and things in their heads, and if you eat them we won't know where to look for the *horhai* because I'm just no good with things like that. I get lost just going around the block, you know?"

Tzi paused.

The guard ran the tip of the skinning knife over Indy's bare chest and ribs, leaving a thin red line indicating the preferred pattern for butchering. Then he invited the other guard to proceed.

"Release them," Tzi said.

The knife had just drawn a trickle of blood along Indy's sternum when the guard was forced to release the pressure on the blade. Muttering, he threw the knife into the bucket and unshackled Indy's wrists.

"Thanks." Indy grinned.

The other guard did the same for Granger.

"Remind me," Granger muttered as he rubbed his wrists, "to kill as many of these buggers as I can before we get out of here."

The guards led them out of the dungeon and up a winding corridor of steps that emerged into a great hall. Black prayer wheels lined both sides of the hall, and whenever one of the monks in the black robes with red cuffs passed, the wheels were spun backward. Instead of prayer staffs, the monks carried with them long black pikes tipped with silver blades. In the center of the hall was a huge caldron on a tripod over a crackling fire, and as the caldron bubbled Indy could catch glimpses of human arms and legs churning in the broth.

At the end of the hall, on a high throne carved from red sandstone, sat a painfully thin figure in a black robe and hood. Indy could not see a face. Beneath the hem of the robe peeked a pair of anti-quated and yellowing shoes called *crakows*, their floppy points looking like bird's feet.

"Let's get on with it," Indy said. "I have places to go."

"Before an audience with the Black One," Tzi said as a trio of monks came forward with wooden bowls of an amber-colored liquid, "you must be pre-pared."

"You can kill me, but I won't drink what's in that pot," Indy swore, and clenched his teeth.

"Don't be so dramatic, Dr. Jones," Tzi said. "The milk of human kindness, as we call it, is reserved for those of us who have pledged our souls to the Dark One. This is merely something to loosen your tongues so that we can get at the truth."

"What is it?" Indy sniffed the bowl that was held in front of him by the monk.

"It is reindeer urine, provided by our friends in nearby Siberia," Tzi explained. "The reindeer feast on the mushroom known as redcap, the fly agaric, and its already potent hallucinogenic qualities are rarefied as they pass through the kidneys of the deer."

"I won't drink it," Indy said.

From behind, Tzi's lieutenant—the same one that had taken them at gunpoint from the camp—jammed a dowel into Indy's mouth and pulled his head back as if he were reining in a horse. The guards held Indy still. He attempted to bite through the wooden dowel, but it was too stout. The monk poured the contents of the bowl over the dowel, and the ammonia-smelling liquid ran down Indy's mouth and pooled in his throat. As the guards held him between them the monk placed his hand over Indy's nose and mouth. Indy was faced with either swallowing the liquid or choking.

Indy swallowed.

The lieutenant laughed.

"Well done, Chang," Tzi told the lieutenant.

The dowel was removed.

"It won't hurt you," Tzi told the others. "Oh, it will upset your stomach and you may have a little vomiting spell when it is over, but you'll experience far more pain if you put up the kind of fight Dr. Jones did."

Granger and Joan swallowed the contents of their bowls.

"This is a nightmare, right?" Joan said. "I mean, I'm asleep in my tent and I'm having this terrible nightmare. Wild dogs, I can believe. But being held prisoner by cannibals and being forced to meet the devil—this has to be a dream. I've had enough of it, and I'm going to wake up now."

"It's no nightmare, Sister," Indy told her.

"Darn," she said. "I'm still here."

"All right," Tzi said. The guards shoved the trio

across the stone floor toward the throne. "On your knees."

"Nope," Indy said. The guards clubbed the backs of his knees, causing his legs to buckle. He hit the floor on his hands and knees.

Granger was treated to the same procedure.

"God forgive me," Joan said as she knelt.

"That is not the one you have to worry about here," Tzi said.

"What now?" Indy asked.

"Stare into the face of the False Lama. Allow the Dark One to enter your soul, to become intimate with the secrets you are careful to hide from the light of day. We are all intrinsically evil; we come from darkness, and to darkness we shall return. The light is merely illusion."

Indy attempted to look anywhere but at the figure on the throne, but he found his eyes being inexorably drawn to the darkness within the hood. In a few moments he was fascinated by the void, and the darkness seemed so complete and reassuring that he forgot why he had been fighting in the first place.

Granger and Joan could not remember, either.

A constellation of stars seemed to gather within the void. With a bony hand enclosed in a red glove, the figure on the throne slowly reached up and pulled back the hood.

Indy gasped as he saw a tangle of red hair spill over the shoulders of the black robe. Alecia smiled at him, her blue eyes burning into his very soul, and she asked who it was that he had expected to meet.

"I don't know," he stammered.

"You don't think love would torture you like this for so long, do you?" she asked. "How could true love be this painful? How could real love be so cursed? No, Junior. But you've known the answer to this one all along. My names are Fear and Desire, and you will never be able to reconcile the two."

"No," Indy said.

"These emotions govern the world. Desire is the bait. Death is the hook. Love is an illusion, a convenient excuse for those who are too weak to take what they really want. You are weak, and so far you've gotten exactly what you deserve: nothing."

"You are not Alecia."

"Of course I am," she said soothingly. "Or don't you remember the tattoo across my back? Or the search for the Philosopher's Stone? Or any of a thousand other things we have shared since that day you walked into the British Museum?"

"Sometimes I hate you," he said.

"Of course you do," she murmured. "Hate is a healthy thing. At least it is passionate. If you loved me, do you think you'd be having those thoughts about that nun? And why shouldn't you hate me? We have shared everything except that one thing which you desire most. And you could have it so easily, and so completely, if only ..."

"If only what?"

"If only you would quit trying to save the world," she replied. "The world doesn't want to be saved. If it did, there wouldn't be a Hitler or a Mussolini. And you know what else? In your heart of hearts, you know that *one person* can't make a difference. It's stupid and useless. And the reason you hate those guys in the starched uniforms so much is because they remind you of yourself. Junior, you would make one perfect Nazi."

Alecia began to laugh.

"I *can* make a difference," Indy said, nearly pleading. "I have to make a difference...."

As Alecia's laughter died out the face in the hood slowly transformed. The blue eyes turned to golden slits and the hair receded into scales.

"I am the Serpent King," a reptilian voiced boomed from the snake's mouth. "The Wyrm Primeval, consciousness engaged in the field of time, the cycle of life, the consumption of the weak by the strong. There is no meaning to life. It is an unending alimentary canal...."

Indy looked away.

"There *is* meaning," he said, his knees shaking.

When he dared to glance back he found himself staring into the orbitals of a grinning crystal skull.

"Tell us about the *horhai*," the skull asked pleasantly in a female voice.

"The triceratops." Indy shook his head in an attempt to understand why he was suddenly talking to the skull.

"Go on."

Indy took a deep breath.

"Continue, I said!"

"Now let me get this straight," Indy said. "You're the all-powerful and all-knowing False Lama, right? Then why are you asking me things that you should already know?"

"Worm bait! How dare you answer my questions with questions."

"Granger," Indy said. "Are you here?"

"Here and there," Granger replied.

"Remember what you asked me to remind you of?"

"Yes," he said.

"Well, it's that time."

Indy spun and grabbed the pike from the surprised monk behind him. He thrust it with all his might toward the throne. The silver blade drove all the way through the robed figure and grated on the sandstone behind. The yellowed *crakows* danced a jig of death.

There was a moment of stunned silence.

"You killed him," one of the guards said, the Thompson dangling from his limp hands. Granger lunged and jerked the gun free and opened fire. The guard jerked like a marionette as the bullets pierced his body, while the other guard dropped his gun and ran.

Then Granger sprayed the interior of the great hall in a wide arc. Slugs chattered over the stone walls, ricocheted from the ceiling, played the big iron cooking pot like a kettledrum, and spun the prayer wheels in the correct direction. Amid this cacophony of righteous anger, the soldiers and monks ran for cover.

Tzi waddled after them.

"They are out of their minds on redcap," he screamed. "Run for your lives!" The fedora fell from his head and landed upside down on the stone floor.

Tzi and all but the unluckiest monks and soldiers managed to find a hiding place, because Granger was having difficulty distinguishing the real targets from the elves and fairies that he saw capering about the chamber.

"Damn imps," he murmured as he clenched his teeth and laid down another barrage.

A brownie scampered out from behind the iron pot and placed its tiny hands on its hips. "You call that shooting?" it scolded. "My fairy godmother can shoot better than that, and she's been dead for four hundred years!"

"Indy!" Granger shouted. "What in the devil are you doing? Get down here and *help* me."

Indy had climbed onto the throne and was sitting on the False Lama's lap. He was attempting, with all of his might, to pull free what he believed was the Crystal Skull.

Then the skull dissolved and the wizened head of a very old man took its place between Indy's hands. He released it, and the head lolled on its shoulders and blood dribbled from one corner of its mouth. He was, Indy could see quite clearly now, simply a dead old man in funny clothes.

Indy jumped down and snatched up his fedora, then picked up the machine gun that the guard had abandoned. He also gathered a pair of hand grenades that hung by clips from the dead guard's belt.

"Which way is out?" Granger asked.

"There's a passage behind the throne," Indy said, "hidden by a wall hanging. It has to lead to the outside, because the wall hanging keeps sighing with the wind."

"Yes, but where does it lead?"

"It's obviously an escape route for the so-called black one when things get too hot." Indy fired a burst at a group of soldiers who had dared to peek around a column. "Since he doesn't need it any longer, I think we should make use of it."

"Go," Granger said, pushing Joan in front of him. "Run. It's our only chance, Sister."

She stumbled into the narrow passage. Granger, who had exhausted the clip, threw down his gun and followed. Indy snatched one of the torches that still blazed beside the throne, sent one last burst into the great hall, then followed.

"That was some stunt you pulled back there," Granger said appreciatively as they raced down the corridor. "You nailed that fakir to the throne as if he were an insect you were mounting for your collection."

"Not much of a plan," Joan said. "But it was effective."

"Tell me, Jones. What did you see?"

"Snakes and skulls," Indy said. "A woman I knew. What did you see?"

"Me?" Granger laughed. "I didn't see anything, of course, except a pathetic old man."

"Sure," Indy said as he ran. "That's why you were raving about imps. So that's what you see in your nightmares, huh? Joan, how about you?"

She stumbled, leaned against the wall for support, and pressed the back of her hand to her mouth. She was breathing heavily.

"Truth?" she asked, fighting for control. "I saw myself."

Then she heaved.

7

THE FLAMING CLIFFS

"Run!" Indy shouted as he pulled the pins on both grenades. He was waiting, his back against the wall and a grenade clenched in each hand, as the slap of the boots on the floor of the stone corridor grew louder.

When it sounded as if the soldiers were a few yards away, Indy tossed the grenades around the corner. The safety clips sprang from the handles as they rolled toward the soldiers.

Indy ran and threw himself upon the floor. Behind him, on the other side of the corner, the explosions brought the roof of the corridor down, blocking the passage.

"Good show," Granger said.

"What?" Indy asked, shaking his head and tugging at his ears.

Granger simply patted his shoulder.

The corridor spilled the trio out onto the desert floor, inside a corral that held Tzi's horses and camels. It was hidden from view by rocks and scrubby trees. The expedition's two trucks were parked inside the fence. A surprised guard looked at the machine gun in Indy's hands, regarded his own single-shot weapon, then threw down the rifle and ran.

"Wise decision," Indy commented.

Granger's truck had a flat tire—owing to some rough treatment by the soldiers—so they climbed into the cab of the other, the one with the flag that bore the museum's logo, and Indy took the wheel.

"I almost forgot," Indy said.

He opened the door and fired the machine gun into the radiator of the other truck.

"Hey," Granger said. "That's expedition equipment."

"You want them hunting us down and killing us with expedition equipment?" Indy asked. Then he reached for the ignition.

"Where are the keys?" he moaned.

Indy hunched beneath the dash and tugged at a spaghetti-like bundle of wires until he found the colors he needed. "I need a knife, a pair of pliers, something," he said. Granger handed him a pair of nail clippers he found in the glove box. Indy quickly stripped the insulation from the wires, but was careful not to break them. Then he twisted the exposed sections of the copper wire together.

When he pressed the starter with his foot, the engine came promptly to life. Indy put the truck in gear and drove through the corral gate and onto the plateau. Horses and camels scattered across the desert behind him.

"Which way?" he asked.

"I haven't the faintest," Granger said, "since I don't know where we've been. The only landmark I recognize is the Flaming Cliffs over there, so I suggest we make for them."

Joan looked behind. The Citadel of the False Lama stood within a huge sandstone outcropping that jutted up from the desert floor. There was no suggestion that the interior of the formation was inhabited.

"How long must it have taken them to carve all of that from the inside?" Joan asked.

"You've got to remember that these are descendants of the people that built the Great Wall," Indy said. "I'm sure it took generations, and that Tzi and his dead friend were just the latest squatters to move in."

Indy looked at the gas gauge, then at the base of the cliffs. He tapped the gauge with his finger, and was alarmed when it went down instead of up.

"I hope we can get there," Indy said. "We're practically running on fumes as it is."

Indy reached beneath the dash and pulled the cable that opened the exhaust cutout. The sound of the engine became a throaty roar, like that of an airplane, as the truck sped across the open desert.

Thirty minutes later the engine coughed and died. Indy took the transmission out of gear and let the truck coast a few meters closer to the Flaming Cliffs before the laws of motion finally brought the wheels to a stop. They were almost to the cliffs, close enough to see the fairytale spires and turrets.

"Any sign behind us?" Indy asked.

"No," Granger said. "But there will be, soon enough."

They got out of the truck; Granger inspected the water bag on the front bumper. It was empty. Everything else had been stripped from the truck.

Indy took down the museum flag, carefully folded it into a tight croissant-shaped package just as he had learned to do in Boy Scouts, and tucked it beneath his shirt.

"We're stranded," Joan wailed. "Out in the middle of this godforsaken country with no water and no provisions. What are we going to do?"

"Now we walk," Indy said, striding off toward the cliffs. "And I suggest you pray as you walk."

Half an hour later Granger stopped and placed his hands on his hips. They were within a quarter mile of the base of the cliffs. "Indy," he said. "Do you think we are still feeling the effects of the mush-room?"

"I don't know," Indy replied. "I don't think so. Why?"

"Look there." Granger pointed midway up the cliffs. "Do you see it? There's a castle in the cliffs, same color as the sandstone." He shielded his eyes with his hands.

"Yes," Indy said.

"I thought it was a figment of my imagination, a remnant of the drug perhaps, but I keep seeing people moving about the tops of the towers and prayer flags fluttering in the wind. Am I insane? It's not the imps again, is it? Or have we died out here in the desert and are those the gates of heaven?"

"Maybe they're the gates of hell," Joan suggested.

"It seems that somebody heard our prayers," Indy said. "The gates have opened and they're sending a party out to meet us. And unless Saint Peter or Old Nick has developed an unusual liking for orange robes, I think that is a procession of lamas."

A tall, athletic-looking white man with a flowing white beard was at the head of the procession of lamas, a staff in one hand, his robes flowing behind him. As the trio met the group Granger stuck out his hand and grinned.

"Dr. Starbuck, I presume."

The man grasped Granger's hand warmly.

"Of course," Starbuck said.

"I am Walter Granger. And this is—"

"Indiana Jones," Starbuck said. "It is a pleasure to meet you again, Dr. Jones. I hope that not too many from your expedition were slaughtered by Tzi and his cannibals."

"We're all that are left," Indy said.

"I'm sorry to hear that," Starbuck said. "I hope you didn't risk all of this just in order to find *me*, because I lost myself quite on purpose. I didn't even tell my daugh—"

Starbuck stared at Joan. A tear was rolling down her dirty cheek. He stepped toward her, took a gourd of water from one of the other monks, and washed her face with his hands.

"Joan?" he asked. "Is that you? Child, I didn't recognize you. Not only do you look older, but you look different somehow. How on earth did you manage to get this far from home?"

Starbuck swept Joan into the folds of his robe while she cried on his shoulder. "Daddy," she said. "I've missed you so much. I thought you were dead. Why didn't you write?"

"It's complicated, my dear," Starbuck said. "Come back with me to the lamastery and it will all be clear to you."

The trio followed Starbuck down corridors that

were spotlessly clean and full of light, with cheerful monks who bowed politely as they passed. Indy noted that their robes were of the same rough weave as the piece of cloth he had ripped from the intruder's robe in New York.

"You joined a lamastery?" Granger asked as they walked. "That's why you disappeared from the face of the earth?"

"I joined nothing," Starbuck declared. "After a while, however, one's old clothes simply wear out, and the robes are convenient. The cloth is made and dyed right here, by the brothers."

He led the way up a spiral staircase into one of the towers. At the top of the staircase, he rapped on the wooden trapdoor.

"It's me, Starbuck."

A monk opened the door. The monk looked strangely familiar to Indy, and when he saw that his robe had been patched, Indy knew why.

The three emerged into a warm room. A trio of braziers, fueled by goat droppings, burned constantly. In the center of the room, on a bed of straw, were three eggs. Each was about the size of a football, and they were a peculiar green color that was tinged with pink.

Indy caught his breath.

"I don't believe it." He marveled. "Am I dreaming?"

"You're not dreaming," Starbuck said. "Although

that was my first reaction as well. It took quite some time to convince myself that these were authentic dinosaur eggs—but that is the undeniable, if somewhat fantastic, truth."

Indy approached the eggs reverently.

"May I touch them?" he asked.

"Of course," Starbuck said. "But do be careful."

With a lump in his throat, Indy walked over and placed his hand gently on one of the eggs. The shell felt leathery and warm. Indy had the dreamlike feeling that he had stepped through a doorway and was actually touching the past.

Granger and Joan crept up next to him and gazed in wonder at the eggs. "I never imagined that they would be so beautiful," Joan said. Then something inside the egg moved and Indy jerked back his hand.

"These eggs are alive!" he exclaimed.

"We hope so," Starbuck said. "They are triceratops eggs. I am not exactly sure of the gestation period, but I am guessing it is eighteen months. That would put us very near to hatching, considering the length of time the mother has been dead."

"The horn," Indy said. "The horn was from the mother."

"Yes," Starbuck said. "I sent it to Joan at the newspaper before fully realizing where the adventure was to lead me. I knew it was a triceratops horn, of course, and I knew that it was from a living animal. Doubtless you surmised the same, Dr. Jones, or else you wouldn't be here."

"Why did you send it?"

"I was so excited that I wanted Joan to share in the find, although I dared not include a written explanation of its significance. Besides, I knew she would be able to deduce that for herself. Only later did I realize that it was a mistake to send such bait to the world, so a couple of the brothers brought it back. I'm sorry that we were too late to keep you from wasting your time."

"Wasting our time?" Granger asked. "We have living dinosaur eggs. I would hardly say we have wasted our time getting here."

For the first time Indy detected a sense of wonder in Granger's voice.

"And they are going to stay here," Starbuck said. "We are desperately trying to keep them alive. But we don't know what temperature is correct, or how often to turn them, or anything really besides keeping them moist. We brought the eggs here so that we could tend them around the clock and so that they would be safe from predators. These eggs, you see— these eggs represent the last of the kind. We knew of no other such living animal besides the mother."

"I don't know whether leaving them here would be a good idea," Granger said. "They must be studied.

They belong in a museum, and we should take them back to New York without delay."

Indy was alarmed at Granger's sudden passion.

Starbuck was about to argue with Granger when Indy, alerted by a sound outside, went to the tower's narrow window.

"I'm afraid there is one other predator that you won't be able to avoid, and I'm afraid we have led him straight to your door," Indy said. "General Tzi. He's out there on the plateau now, planning to lay siege to the lamastery."

Starbuck joined Indy at the window.

"We'll have to get the eggs out of here," Starbuck said.

"Good God," Granger said. "They're unlimbering a howitzer down there. Tzi means business."

"I'll alert the brothers," Starbuck said.

"Professor," Indy said. "Just one more question. I thought I heard you say that you sent the horn to Joan's paper, but that couldn't be right. Didn't you mean you sent the horn to her order?"

"Her order? Order of what?" Starbuck asked as he opened the trapdoor and began to climb down. "Joan is a reporter for the *Kansas City Star.*"

"Sorry," Joan said. "I've been meaning to tell you, but I just didn't know how."

"I think I'll see if Professor Starbuck and the brothers need any help," Granger improvised. "It seems you kids have a few things to work out."

He left the tower also.

"Why the masquerade?" Indy asked.

"Well, if I had told you I was a reporter, would you have taken me as seriously?" Joan asked. "I wanted to find my father, and I knew you were the right man to help me do it, but I didn't have the kind of resources necessary to mount such an expedition. I figured I had to get the resources of the museum behind me, so I just played dumb and made it seem like yours and Brody's idea."

Indy's face was red with rage.

"The fact that you knew you were onto the story of the century—no, of the *millennium*—probably didn't hurt, either," he said. "How could I have been so stupid? The constant questions about this or that, your demand to accompany us all of the way...it all makes perfect sense, now."

"He is still my father," Joan said. "And I had a desperate desire to find him. And I didn't lie when I talked about my family's belief in the basic goodness of humanity. But my editors at the *Star* laughed at me when I suggested they send me to Mongolia, so I had to come up with something to get here. The habit was a Halloween costume I had worn to a party earlier in the week, so I decided to use it. I can see now how wrong that was, but it made sense at the time."

"It's called rationalization," Indy said.

"I know what I did was wrong," she said.

"And you seemed to enjoy it," Indy said. "You played the slutty nun to the hilt. You seemed to like it so much that I'll bet it was hard for you to leave the costume behind."

"I was lonely and I was scared much of the time," Joan said. "I'm just human, you know."

"Oh, you're something more than human. Were you going to tell me that you weren't really a nun before or after you got me into the sack, Sister?"

She looked at him.

"Sorry, it's a hard habit to break." She laughed in spite of herself.

"Look, Dr. Jones. We both know you would have gone on this expedition whether I was a nun, a newspaper reporter, or had two heads and purple hair. So what's the damage?"

She took off his fedora, draped her arms around his neck, and kissed him. Hard.

Indy pulled himself away.

"Sorry," he said. "I don't give my heart to liars. Besides, I'm in love with somebody else."

"You mean that witch who dumped you?"

"Did you say witch or—"

"You heard me," Joan said. "I can't believe you're carrying a torch for her after all she's put you through, and obviously I don't know the half of it. But I can gather enough from the conversations you've had with Brody and Granger that you're way too good for her."

"You don't understand," Indy protested.

"And what is it that I need to understand about Indiana Jones?" she asked.

"That I'm a hopeless, raving romantic," he said. "That I keep my word to my friends. That I don't sleep around when I'm in love with somebody else. That I don't lose my values just because I'm a few thousand miles from home. That there are things in this world which science can't explain but which just maybe the human heart can. And that I would never, ever date a girl who dresses like a nun."

The first shell from the howitzer blasted a hole in the wall of the lamastery the size of a bushel basket.

"Time to abandon ship," Indy said. "We can't hold off Tzi's army with one machine gun and five rounds of ammunition."

"If only we had more weapons," Granger said.

"We don't, so we'll have to make a run for it," Indy said.

"Even if we had weapons," Starbuck said, "I would not resort to killing. That would make us no better than the animals beyond the gates."

"Sometimes it's better to be a living animal," Granger said, "than a dead philosopher. If you find some guns, you let me know."

"Professor," Indy said. "I'm sorry, but I think

that Tzi is going to blow this monastery to bits. You need to tell the brothers to come with us."

"They'll be fine," Starbuck insisted as he lifted a dinosaur egg from the bed of straw and slipped it into Indy's satchel. "They are used to playing this cat-and-mouse game with Tzi and his men, and they will scatter when we leave. I am hopeful that it will buy us some time."

"Where are we going?" Joan asked.

"Through a narrow passage in the cliffs," Starbuck said. "There is a valley beyond which has been untouched by time. We must be careful, because the path is perilous, and we must make sure that Tzi's men do not follow us into the valley. I only wish there were another place that we could take refuge, but I am afraid it is our last hope—and the last hope of our three little ones."

Starbuck placed another of the eggs in a straw-filled leather pouch and handed it to Joan, who slung it beneath her shoulder like a purse.

"Let me," Granger offered as Starbuck placed the last egg into a pouch. "I don't have anything to do with my hands, and you're going to be busy leading the way. I promise that I'll take good care of it."

"Hey," Indy said, and whistled at Granger. "Nice purse."

"You should talk," Granger returned. "You've carried that little bag of yours around the world three or four times, I understand."

"This," Indy said, "is a satchel. *That,* however, is a purse."

"All right, then," Starbuck said, taking up his staff. He rapped on the back wall of the tower, breaking away the plaster over a hidden passage. When they were gone, the monks had instructions to patch over the doorway before abandoning the lamastery.

Starbuck took up a bundle of torches, lit one from the nearest brazier, and turned to face the group. "To the promised land," he said, then entered the passage.

"Religion *does* run in the family," Joan snapped as she cut in front of Indy to catch up with her father.

"Apparently so does insanity," Indy muttered.

Granger was the last to file into the passage, and as he did so, a shell from the howitzer hit the tower, blowing the top off and spilling the braziers onto the plank floor. It also drove a splinter from the ceiling into the leather bag that Granger carried, and a trickle of amniotic fluid began to mark the trail behind them.

8

THE HAPPY VALLEY

"This passage was staked by the ancients, and it is full of traps for the unwary," Starbuck called back. "I'm sure you've experienced nothing like it before."

Indy smiled.

The path led deep into the mountain, and the first obstacle they encountered was a narrow footbridge of natural stone that crossed a gaping chasm.

"Be careful," Starbuck warned as he carefully put one foot in front of the other, like a tightrope walker. "This abyss has no bottom."

"Any chasm that is too deep from one to easily see the bottom," Granger remarked, "is said to be bottomless." He picked up a stone and, when he was in the center of the bridge, let it drop from his outstretched hand. He waited.

Thirty seconds later he was still waiting.

"Let's see," Indy calculated. "Given the law of falling bodies, that rock must have fallen...that would be 16.08 times 30 squared...around 14,400 feet, or nearly three miles by now. I'd call *that* bottomless, wouldn't you?"

"We just didn't hear it," Granger said, and moved on.

The natural bridge ended at a spectacular staircase hewn from the rocks, and the staircase led into the mountain for several hundred feet and then began to serpentine along the rim of a gorge. They could see all the way to the bottom of the gorge, because it was filled with molten lava.

"I didn't think we were near any active volcanoes here," Joan said. The heat had plastered her hair against her face, and the weight of the egg was beginning to make her shoulder ache.

"It is part of the intricate ecological system of the valley where we are going," Starbuck said. "The ground and the water there are warm, defying even the Gobi's harshest winters."

"Sounds like a paradise," Joan said.

"It is," Starbuck concurred. "I hope it stays that way."

The staircase ended at a precipice. A heavy rope was tied around the base of a stalagmite, and the rope disappeared into darkness beyond the edge. The river of molten rock flowed far below.

"Now for the hard part," Starbuck announced.

"It's been easy so far?" Joan asked.

"We must pull ourselves across on this rope."

Starbuck handed the torch to Granger. Then, to demonstrate, he sat on the edge of the precipice, grasped the rope with both hands, and swung out. He swayed there for a moment, then began to swing his legs up, and finally grasped the rope with his ankles.

"This is the best way to cross," he said. "Pull yourself along, hand over hand."

"What do I do with the torch?" Granger asked.

"Give it to me. I'll carry it in my teeth," Indy said.

Joan was next. She looped the bag containing the egg around her neck, then confidently grasped the rope. She swung her legs up, and began to pull herself across.

"My hands hurt," she complained halfway across.

"Keep going, Sister," Indy said behind her.

"They're bleeding."

The blood on her palms made the rope dangerously slick, and Joan's pace slowed to a few inches each stroke. But when she tried to hurry up so the ordeal would be over with and the pain in her hands would end, she lost her grip on the rope entirely.

She bobbed upside down by her ankles, the leather pouch hanging by her chin.

"The egg!" Indy shouted. His words were muf-
fled because of the torch in his mouth.

"What do I do?" Joan mumbled.

"Don't talk," Indy ordered. He looped an arm
around the rope and took the torch out of his
mouth. "Everybody, stop. Don't bounce the rope.
Joan, can you reach the egg?"

"No," she said. "The strap's too long."

"Okay, listen carefully," Indy said. "I want you
to very gently reach down and grasp the strap.
Firmly. You got it?"

"Yes," Joan said. "But the blood is rushing to my
head and I'm getting really dizzy."

"Slowly, raise the pouch."

"Okay," she said.

"Slowly!"

"I am!"

"Stop there," Indy said. "With your fingertips,
try to tuck the egg back into the pouch. It's on the
edge, so don't jostle it."

"All right," Joan said.

Her fingertips touched the leathery surface of the
edge. Just as she nearly had the girth of the egg
safely pushed back over the lip of the pouch, the
rope jerked as several of its strands separated.

The egg bounced out of the pouch. It fell for several seconds and then struck the lava river with a
hiss.

"Oh my God!" Joan said. "I'm sorry, I tried—"

"It wasn't your fault," Indy said. "There's too many of us on this rope. We need to get to the other side, as quickly as we can."

"But Indy," Joan protested. "I can't reach the rope with my arms. I don't have the strength. And Indy, I am really dizzy and I am really tired."

"Hang on," Indy said.

He moved quickly across to where she hung. Then, switching the torch again and looping his left arm around the rope once more, he extended his right arm toward her.

She struggled against her own weight and reached up with her left hand. Their fingertips brushed, then Indy had her hand in his and hauled her up.

The rope shook again as more strands separated.

Joan started to cry.

"Let's go," Indy said. "Don't worry about it. It was absolutely not your fault. We've got two whole eggs left."

"Correction," Granger said as he dipped his fingers in the fluid dripping from his pouch. "We've got your whole egg left, but I'm afraid mine's been scrambled somehow. Actually, it doesn't smell half bad."

"This is worse than the egg toss at the county fair," Indy said. "And Granger? If I don't get out of this thing, please do me a favor and don't deliver the eulogy at my memorial service. I don't want you sticking me with a fork."

"Wouldn't dream of it, old boy. Brown eyes, you know."

Once they all had reached the other side, Indy took out his sheath knife and hacked through the rest of the rope. He watched the frayed end as it fell into the darkness.

"That will make it a little harder for Tzi," Indy said.

"If he comes," Starbuck suggested.

"No," Granger put in. "*When* he comes."

"But what if we want to go back?" Joan asked.

"We'll make ourselves a slingshot," Indy said.

"Come," Starbuck said. "We are almost there."

In another three hundred yards, the passage ended in a large cavern. They slid down a clay slope to the floor, then walked out of the mouth of the cavern into a sunlit valley.

Indy blinked. The valley was filled with pine trees, broad leafy ferns, and a number of flowering plants that he could not identify. A girl of about eighteen or twenty, bare from the waist up and wearing a skirt made of antelope skin, came over to Indy and placed a garland of the unusual flowers around his neck. Then she laughed and ran away.

"Welcome," Starbuck said, "to the Stone Age."

"These are the Dune Dwellers," Starbuck explained as he laid the remaining dinosaur egg on a bed of ferns inside a little wooden shrine that had quickly been fashioned for it. "Or at least they are cousins of the Dune Dwellers whose jewelry you found outside the Flaming Cliffs. They revere the *allergorhai-horhai,* the triceratops, just as the Plains Indians worshiped the buffalo. It has been the center of their life for countless generations. Only, the dinosaurs are all gone now, except for our single egg."

"But this valley," Indy said. "How has it survived untouched for so long? This isn't *like* the late Cretaceous. This is it."

"Well, you saw what it took to get here," Starbuck said. "It is protected by the Flaming Cliffs, of course. And this area is so remote. These people have been cut off for several thousand years from the rest of the world. A stray traveler has obviously gotten through from time to time, judging from Mongolian folklore about the *horhai,* but that of course can be dismissed as myth. Actually, the introduction of an occasional stranger has helped these people survive by adding to the genetic stock. It is a common genetic stock and apparently hasn't upset things too badly."

"How many are they?" Granger asked.

"Forty-six," Starbuck said. "That includes about twenty-five adults. There are a dozen children, and the rest are old people. Both the children and

the elderly are cared for by the community as a
whole."

"I wish I had a camera," Joan said. "This place is
unbelievable. Can you imagine the sensation a story
with photos would make?"

"That is precisely why I am glad that you don't
have a camera," Starbuck said. "There is nothing
that would destroy these people more than being
discovered. There would be an airstrip in this valley
in a matter of weeks, and then what would we
have?"

"But wouldn't they be happier?" Granger
asked. "Surely disease takes its toll on these people. Wouldn't the modern world be a blessing for
them?"

"No." Starbuck was emphatic. "It would be a
curse. They have been isolated for so long that they
are free of the diseases that most modern cultures
spread. Smallpox, for example. You've all been vac-
cinated? Good. It spread through the Native
American tribes like wildfire after the invasion of
America."

"Invasion?" Granger asked.

"I have a deep conviction, Mr. Granger, that the
American Indians would have fared much better
had their continent not been discovered by the
Europeans. Our Dune Dwellers here are the same.
Look at them! Laughing and playing like children.
They are well fed and free of most of the diseases

that ravage humanity, and they live in a valley that is perpetually temperate. The lamastery has guarded this valley for hundreds of years, and they will set a broken bone when needed or assist with a difficult childbirth, but otherwise there is a strict prohibition against contact."

"Incredible," Granger said. "I don't know whether to pity these people or to envy them."

"Why the confusion?" Starbuck asked. "The People do not have to work for their survival. All they need is here. And they have never been introduced to the idea of sin."

"It's the Garden of Eden," Joan said.

"Pardon me, Professor," Granger said. "I appreciate your views, but what about your responsibility to science. Aren't you being selfish, keeping all this to yourself as your own paradise?"

"I believe I can best serve that duty by remaining here," Starbuck said. "I have taken voluminous notes since I first arrived six months ago, and I intend to continue. Why, I have just scratched the surface of their language and their way of life. I don't even know what to call them. They call themselves the *canobi,* which simply means 'the People.' They have no word or concept for what a stranger is. They make no distinction between themselves and others. To them, we are all part of the tribe—we've just been away so long they can't remember us. That's why they have no fear."

"Original innocence," Joan said.

"What we are dealing with is the source of all cultures—all of us sprang from people like the Dune Dwellers, if not the Dune Dwellers themselves. In the geological scheme of things, modern man has just left this happy valley. Imagine what a boon to the world it would be if we could get a glimpse inside those Neolithic heads and find out what makes *us* tick. There is much to be done, Dr. Jones, and so very little time to do it."

"What do you mean?" Indy asked.

"Time is running out for this happy valley," Starbuck told him. "It is inevitable that the rest of the world will discover them. When that happens, the opportunity to study them in their natural environment will be over. Then this will no longer be the Stone Age—it will be just another backwater blemish on the face of the twentieth century."

"Say," Granger interjected, examining the contents of his pouch. "What are we going to do about this ruined egg? Is there any way we can preserve it?"

"I'm afraid not," Starbuck said. "They spoil rather quickly."

"What a waste." Granger shook his head.

"Perhaps not," Starbuck said. "The People consider the eggs a great delicacy, and I have had a devil of a time keeping them from making Neolithic omelettes out of our three. They also think there is something mystical about the consumption of the dinosaur eggs which confers vitality upon them and ensures survival for the species. Since there's nothing we can do to save this egg, let's cook it up and put their superstition to the test."

"Bravo," Granger said.

Starbuck patted the egg, covered it with a frond, and rose.

"My hope is to buy the People a little more time. In a few more years—in a few more decades, if we're lucky—it will be all over. But until that happens, I will remain here, living and studying these people, and that baby triceratops that's about to hatch. Then, when the world comes bursting in, clamoring for the story—the story will be ready to be told."

"What about Joan?" Indy asked.

She had left the conversation to wander among the People. A slim young man with a shock of black hair was following behind her, a bouquet of Cretaceous buds in his hand.

"She will have to make up her own mind," Starbuck said. "One photo, one wire dispatch, will prove the happy valley's undoing. But I am not her master. Only her father."

"There's something I'm curious about," Indy said. "That girl that greeted us seemed to be extremely friendly. Pardon my asking, but how intimate are you with these people?"

"They call me grandfather." Starbuck laughed. "And I feel grandfatherly toward them, as well. Besides, I am too old to adopt their ways. And no one could take the place of Joan's mother, who died in childbirth."

"Pull up a seat, old man," Granger said.

It was after the feast of the dinosaur-egg omelette that evening, and Granger was sitting contentedly on a rock, smoking his pipe. Indy sat next to him and plucked up a blade of grass and began to chew on it.

"That egg was delicious," Granger began.

"Didn't eat any of it," Indy said. "Reminded me of when I was a kid and I'd get an egg at breakfast that had an embryo in it. I'd be sick for days just thinking about it. I just wish there was some way we could have preserved it—what I wouldn't give for a little bit of formaldehyde—but it was useless."

"Why, we could make a fortune if we could just get our hands on some more of those eggs. We could serve 'em up at one-thousand-dollar-a-plate dinner parties. Granger's famous chicken-fried dinosaur. Has a nice ring to it, doesn't it?"

"Will you be serious for a moment?"

"I was only partially joking," Granger said. "You

know, that egg does belong on the outside. It is much too valuable to leave in this lost valley, where it runs the risk of being eaten by the inhabitants.... What is it, Jones? You look like you've gotten your marching orders."

"In a way," Indy said. "I went back into the cavern a few minutes ago, and I could hear Tzi's dogs sniffing out our trail on the other side of the rope gorge. Starbuck is wrong about how much time these people have. It isn't a matter of decades or years...it's a matter of hours. And when Tzi finds this valley, he will destroy everything in it."

"So what do we do?" Granger asked.

"I'm leaving," Indy said. "Going to try to put Tzi off the trail, to lead him far away from here and into the steppes. To do anything to get him away from this valley."

"You always were the idealist," Granger said. "Actually, I had hoped to stay here for a little while. We've been here only a few hours. It's a pleasant valley and I haven't even had time to meet these people, to learn their names and so forth. Some of them seem quite clever, actually. Not to mention beautiful."

"We can't know these people," Indy said. "They are wonderful children and we are big awkward adults. Besides, what good are we doing ourselves if we stay here? How are we supposed to fight when

Tzi finally comes down out of that cavern with his dogs and his soldiers?"

"We fight like we always have," Granger said. "We've managed to save our skins through a little tenacity and a lot of luck enough times to know that you never know how these things will turn out. One should never give up. It's better to die on your feet than on your knees."

"Okay," Indy said. "Say a miracle happens and we win. We train these people to use spears and clubs and we drive Tzi out of this valley by force. We'll still have lost, because we'll have taught these people how to kill."

"They'll learn that soon enough anyway."

"I want to stay," Indy said. "I've wanted to stay from the minute I set foot here and that girl with the wonderful eyes gave me the flowers. When I asked Starbuck if he was intimate with these people, it wasn't just out of curiosity. I wanted to plan a life here. No more fighting, no more curses, and especially no more jackbooted fascists. But I can't. For me, it's wrong."

"Jones, you're giving me a headache."

"I'll make it simple for you." Indy stood up and shouldered the Thompson and its five-round clip. "I'm going to do what I can. You can come with me or not."

"All right," Granger said. "But there's just two things. Our discussion on the last triceratops egg is far from over. I still think it belongs in a museum, or if it hatches, in some kind of zoo."

"Okay," Indy said. "We'll talk that over when the time comes. What's the second thing?"

"I get the gun," Granger said.

9

THUNDER CHILD

Indy looked over the lip of the ravine and across the steppe with red-rimmed eyes. His gaze took in every feature, each rock and scrubby tree, anxious for any sign of Tzi.

For the last week he and Granger had played a desperate game of hide-and-seek with Tzi and his soldiers, leading them away from the valley and ever farther into the steppes. In Granger's capable hands, the five rounds in the Thompson had accounted for five soldiers, soldiers who had wandered too far from the rest of Tzi's army and had paid for the mistake with their lives. From those careless soldiers came a little food, some water, a Mauser rifle, and the Webley revolver that had been taken from Indy in what now seemed like a geologic epoch gone by.

Indy had only a few rounds left for the Webley—

a handful in a jacket pocket and the six in the cylinder. Mongol horsemen were among the best riders on earth, and they would prove difficult targets with a handgun.

Granger was in even worse shape. The box magazine on the Mauser held ten shells and his ammunition belt was empty.

"We're out of water," Granger announced. "We ate the last of that pitiful rodent meat yesterday." He removed his safari hat and sleeved sweat from his brow.

Indy watched shadows lengthening below a rocky escarpment as the sun lowered. "I suppose it would be pointless to ask if you have any good news."

"What?" Granger asked.

"Good news," Indy repeated. "Do you have any?"

"These little horses are spent," Granger told him, replacing his hat. "We've ridden them too hard. I tried to warn you, Jones. As always, you wouldn't listen to me."

There was a furtive movement that may have been an antelope—or one of Tzi's soldiers. Indy studied the spot carefully when he saw the movement again, and now he was certain it was someone creeping slowly toward them.

"They're out there," he added, "crawling this way. Still out of pistol range."

Granger examined the spot where Indy was looking. "I see it now. If he's one of Tzi's scouts, they'll send their wild dogs in for us first." He raised his Mauser, working sweaty fingers on the pistol grips.

"This is a bad place to make a last stand," Indy said.

"You're developing a rather annoying habit of stating the obvious with unnecessary clarity, Jones. I don't need the help of a college professor to calculate that twenty cartridges won't be enough to kill about a hundred wild dogs and fifty Mongol cannibals."

Indy's sorrel pony pricked up its ears and turned its head toward the outcrop, sensing something.

"They're coming for us now." Indy reached for the Webley tucked into his belt, feeling the hairs on the back of his neck rise.

"Do you think he'll send the dogs in first?" he asked. "I hope they don't send the dogs. I'd like a shot at Tzi."

"Count on the dogs," Granger said.

"You're a comfort," Indy said.

The sorrel snorted once more, bowing its neck and fighting the lead that was tied to the trunk of a scrubby little tree. The eyes of both horses were wild. They had smelled the dog pack approaching.

"What about the horses?" Indy asked.

"What about them?" Granger returned. "The dogs will get them, too. They'll rip open their bellies first and spill their intestines on the ground. Then they'll take their time finishing them off."

"Let 'em go," Indy said.

Granger agreed. "Of course. I don't suppose we have any more need of them. And it could buy us some time if they pursue the ponies and leave us alone."

Granger put down the Mauser and went over to where the horses were tied. He untied the sorrel, looped the reins around the pommel so they wouldn't become tangled beneath its hooves, then released the animal. It reared and then took off across the steppe, its hooves flashing.

Then he did the same with the other horse.

Indy looked around. The plain was clear for several hundred yards on either side of the gully. He put his attention back on the escarpment where he'd seen the shadow move.

"Do you think it's better here?" Indy asked. "Or down there?"

"I'd rather stay here." Granger returned and took up the Mauser. Then he picked up a handful of sand and sifted it through his fingers. "Is it worth dying for, to say with our last breath that we helped hatch the world's only living triceratops?"

"There are worse things to die for," Indy replied. "Besides, it's more than that. It's Joan and Starbuck we're talking about, too, and the Dune Dwellers—

or whatever they call themselves. Do you think Tzi would spare any of them?"

"If we could just have gotten that egg back to New York, we'd be credited with the greatest scientific find of all time," Granger said. "Imagine what a sensation if it actually hatched. Instead, I'm going to wind up in a Mongol stew."

"Relax," Indy told him. "It's only your heart they eat, and yours is so black it will probably give Tzi a bad case of indigestion. Wait, I see something...."

An animal skulked along the base of the same rock formation. "A dog," he said quietly, with growing concern. "Isn't it ironic that the animal I like best in the world is going to be the cause of my death?"

"I always figured an animal would get me in the end." Granger rubbed his damaged ear as he spoke. "A leopard, an elephant. Perhaps a lion. Wouldn't that be a grand way to go? But a dog? You've never seen a dog mounted on the wall of anybody's book-lined study. And a dog doesn't even make a decent hatband."

Another wild dog crept over the rocks behind the first.

"It would be extremely fortuitous if that brigand Khan would show up about now." Granger paused listening. "Here they come."

"Good," Indy said. "I'm tired of waiting."

Spread out across the horizon, mounted Mongol warriors galloped toward them, surrounded by packs of running dogs. Indy didn't bother counting dogs or horsemen, not with only a dozen bullets to his name.

"Jones," Granger said.

"Yeah?"

"Nobody ever expects to find themselves in a situation like this, but I'm glad that . . . What I mean is that there's nobody I'd rather . . . Dammit, Jones, you know what I'm trying to say."

"The feeling's mutual," Indy said.

Mounted on a bow-backed chestnut stallion, General Tzi and his lieutenant, Chang, rode along the bottom of the draw flanked by dozens of Mongol tribesmen carrying an assortment of weapons. Most were single-shot muskets, but there were a few men who cradled repeating rifles in the crooks of their arms. Trotting around them, a pack of wild dogs yelped and snarled at one another as if they awaited the command to begin feeding.

"We're doomed," Granger whispered softly. "There are too many of them. They've got us surrounded."

"Things could be worse, I suppose," Indy remarked dryly.

"How's that?" Granger asked, searching Indy's face.

"They could be carrying baskets of snakes."

Indy studied Tzi's rotund face, and then looked at Chang's hooded eyes and hawk-beak nose, a Fu Manchu mustache decorating his chin.

"Those two guys are really ugly," he added, bringing the barrel of his Webley up, his finger curling around the trigger.

"What they're planning to do to us will be ugly," Granger shot back. "If I get a chance I'll take a shot at General Tzi as soon as he gets in range. If I allow for the wind, I might be able to drop him. That ought to take the wind out of their sails!"

"He won't ride that close," Indy promised. "The fat bugger is too smart for that. He'll let his dogs do the dirty work."

"Too many dogs," Granger observed, with a hunter's understanding for wild animals attacking in packs.

"They'll come at us from all directions." Indy swallowed hard. "Our guns won't scare them off."

"Not the way you shoot, anyway," Granger agreed.

"Would you quit picking on my shooting," Indy snapped. "It may not be fancy, but it gets the job done."

"Indy," Granger said. "Save two bullets for that famous shooting of yours."

"Why?"

"For us," Granger said. "Our situation looks hopeless."

"I'll never be *that* hopeless," Indy said. "If they want me dead, they're going to have to fight for the opportunity to kill me." He readied his pistol.

"Get down, Jones!" Granger cried. But Indy's attention was riveted on a solitary animal well behind the riders and the other dogs. Its nose was to the ground. It was a dog of unusual size, with blue eyes, and it behaved as if it were tracking General Tzi and his men rather than being a part of the pack. It was difficult to tell at this distance, but it seemed that it had only one ear.

"If I didn't know better I'd swear that's Loki," Indy muttered.

But he wasn't given time for a closer inspection of the dog. A Mongol warrior wheeled his pony and sent it lunging down the side of the ravine. Indy drew back the hammer of the Webley. The warrior drummed his heels into the horse's ribs and charged, bending low over his black pony's neck with a carbine in his hands.

"This fool is committing suicide," Granger said, sighting down the barrel of his Mauser.

Suddenly the rider disappeared. A split second later he was hanging off the far side of his horse only inches from the ground, with one foot suspended in a length of rope, peering between his pony's flying legs, and it seemed he was almost smiling at them.

"What the hell?" Granger wondered, scowling.

Indy relaxed a little. This was showmanship, not an attack. "It's called the Cossack drag. I saw it once in southern Russia. General Tzi wants his men to put on an exhibition before he kills us so we'll be scared of him. I figure he won't kill us both until we tell him where to find that egg, so he aims to try to frighten us into a real talkative mood."

"I can't shoot him without killing his horse," Granger said, lowering his gun barrel when the rider was hidden again behind his pony. "A nine-millimeter slug won't pierce that much tissue and bone. I'd be wasting a bullet."

The Mongol galloped past them before he steered his speeding pony away. Indy glanced back to the ravine, noticing the absence of the one-eared dog he'd seen a moment earlier. Then he turned his attention to Tzi and Chang.

"Looks like General Tzi has gained even more weight," Indy commented. "Nothing like a diet of human hearts to put some fat around a hungry warlord's belly."

"Good grief, Jones. What a lousy time for bad jokes."

The warrior returned to the pack. He rode over to Tzi and said something while motioning with his hands. Tzi nodded, then turned a baleful stare toward Indy and Granger. For a moment he sat on his horse as if he were cast in bronze.

"They'll really be coming this time," Granger said. "The show is over."

"You're beginning to irritate me with all your whimpering, Granger. We're not dead yet." Indy examined the pack of dogs again. "I'd almost swear I saw Loki a minute ago, only I know it can't be the same dog. He would have found his way back to us long before now if he could."

When Indy glanced over his shoulder, he saw a line of mounted tribesmen beginning to form a loose circle around them. It was, he had to admit, a fearsome sight the way they were spread out with their dogs trotting at their horses' heels. Rifle barrels and swords glistened in the afternoon sun. Granger was sweating profusely when he saw the circle tightening. There appeared to be no escape.

"This is what I get for listening to you, Jones," Granger snapped angrily. "If things were left up to me, I'd be on my way to New York now. Being friends with you will cost me my life, and all because of your stupid sentimentality over a reptilian egg."

Indy was stunned by Granger's sudden outburst.

Before he could answer, a swirl of dust cloaked the approach of General Tzi and his army to the rim of the ravine. Groups of wild dogs scrambled everywhere, eyes fixed on the two men at the center of a tightening circle.

Indy placed his back against Granger's.

"Maybe it was stupid sentimentality, but Starbuck may give the world a gift so rare it could rewrite everything we know about the past," he said over his shoulder. "But I will ignore your bad temper because of the years of friendship we've shared. And I hate to interrupt this lovers' tiff, but try to kill as many of the dogs as you can. Maybe a few gunshots will bring someone to our rescue before it's too late."

"You call that a *plan*?" Granger snarled over his shoulder. "If you hadn't noticed, it's much too late for that. I should never have listened to you in the first place, Jones."

General Tzi raised his hand, making ready to signal a charge toward Granger and Indy. A silence spread around the far-flung circle of warriors. More tribesmen drew curved swords, reflecting rays of brilliant sunlight. Most of the dogs stopped barking as though they knew what would happen next.

"Dr. Jones!" Tzi shouted. "How does it feel to know that you will die now at the hands of the great General Tzi?" His voice was hard to hear in the wind.

"Not all that bad, actually!" Indy replied at the top of his lungs. "We were just saying that today was about as good as any to dine on fresh dog meat! And I'm saving my last bullet for *you*, you fat old—"

"It is time!" Tzi cried, giving Chang a wicked half grin.

A dog came out of the ravine, trotting closer to Tzi's pony in a curious way, limping slightly as if some old wound made it lame. Indy saw the dog when it broke into a run. There were so many dogs around them that none of Tzi's soldiers noticed it at first.

General Tzi's massive head turned and his piglike eyes grew wide. He pointed toward the running dog and shouted a command. Chang drew his sword, but he was too late. The dog was already in the air, teeth bared.

"That's Loki," Indy whispered disbelievingly, blinking his eyes to make sure of what he saw. "It can't be. . . ."

Tzi tried to block the dog's open jaws by bringing up both arms and twisting his head, but Loki landed in the saddle with Tzi. Razor-sharp fangs dug into the flesh of Tzi's right cheek, while the dog's springing leap knocked the overfed warlord from his chestnut's back. He toppled heavily to the ground, landing with a thud and a groan as blood spewed from his face. Loki backed away snarling, a chunk of bloody tissue dangling from his jaws.

Chang shouted to other warriors as he came at Loki with the gleaming sword, swinging his blade in a deadly arc toward the Alsatian. But the scent of blood triggered a far more frenzied reaction among Tzi's wild dogs. First two, then half a dozen animals jumped on him, tearing at his bleeding wound while the warlord began to kick and scream. More wild dogs landed atop Tzi's fat belly to bite him wherever spilled blood had fallen.

"Good Lord," Granger muttered.

The entire pack charged him now, snapping and yelping in a feeding frenzy. Twenty dogs, then a few more, nipped and chewed upon Tzi's flesh, tearing off his clothing and pieces of skin. Tzi thrashed back and forth on the ground, shrieking with pain, windmilling his arms and legs. Indy saw Loki trot off a short distance, then the shepherd sat on its haunches and watched while General Tzi was ripped to pieces by his own dogs.

None of the other Mongols came to the general's rescue.

Chang backed his pony away, staring down at the feeding dog pack as he sheathed his sword. A wild dog tore off Tzi's left foot and slunk away to chew on a morsel of flesh and bones. When Chang saw this he shouted to his tribesmen, but because of the din made by so many snarling animals, Indy couldn't hear what he said.

"Good Lord," Granger mouthed again breathlessly. The attack had come so fast he hadn't had time to speak. "That was Loki who knocked General Tzi off his horse, wasn't it?"

"That was him all right." Indy sighed, examining his beloved dog's coat from a distance. "Who needs bullets when you can rely on the loyalty of a dog? I can't remember when I was so glad to have a friend show up."

Wild dogs continued feeding on Tzi's carcass, only now there was no movement from him, save for a jerk or a twist when a dog bit off a hunk of meat, nor were there more of his eerie, bloodcurdling screams. Blood lay everywhere in dark crimson pools, quickly lapped up by smaller canines. A speckled female ripped open Tzi's belly, seeking his internal organs, burying her head inside his rib cage.

More Mongol warriors rode slowly toward Chang, sheathing their swords, lowering their rifles, no longer paying any attention to Granger and Indy.

"They're having some sort of conference," Granger observed. "It must have to do with what they plan to do with us." He put his pistol inside his belt to watch what was going on. "Do you suppose they'll let us go free?"

Loki abandoned the melee and trotted in Indy's direction.

"Damn, what a beautiful sight," Indy said under his breath, ignoring Granger's question, hoping Loki could get to him before Chang or any of the others exacted revenge for what he had done to General Tzi. Indy noticed Loki's limp, and all the old scars covering the dog's body, and a few new scars, and of course the missing ear.

Loki walked up, wagging his tail. A trace of

blood remained on the dog's upper lip until a long pink tongue flicked it away.

"I thought you were dead," Indy said as he hugged the dog's neck and stared into the Alsatian's mysterious, almost human blue eyes. Loki made a sound in his throat, a happy noise.

"Good to see you," Indy whispered, then Loki began to pant. "You look like you've been half starved. . . . What's the matter, can't bring yourself to eat what they feed the others?"

A commotion at the end of the ravine halted Indy's reunion with the dog. Chang, for reasons Indy couldn't understand, began to lead his warriors away. The nomads who just minutes ago had formed a deadly circle around them reined their ponies, starting back in the direction from which they had come, taking their dog packs with them. They rode off in a cloud of pale sandstone dust, leaving Indy and Granger to themselves.

"Why, they aren't going to kill us after all!" Granger exclaimed. Some of Tzi's wild dogs chewed on bits of his dismembered carcass for a moment more, until a tribesman whistled sharply, ending the animals' feeding. One brown cur carried Tzi's bloody severed head toward the ravine, until a spotted dog attacked the brown's flank savagely over the prize. Tzi's fleshless skull now appeared to be grinning as it rolled over the lip of the ravine like a misshapen ball.

"The nomads never wanted us in the first place," Indy said. "It was Tzi and the False Lama who had them under their spell. Now that they're both dead, maybe they'll forget about us."

"Maybe," Granger said. "But I think we just got lucky."

"Yeah," Indy said. "And our luck is a blue-eyed dog."

"We could use a little more luck to retrieve those horses," Granger said. "That was a damn fool idea, letting them go like that. We have to get back to the valley. Our egg is waiting on us."

"It isn't our egg," Indy warned. "It belongs where it is, in the valley. It's too important to history for any disputes over ownership."

"Now hold on a minute!" Granger complained. "You and I saved that egg from certain destruction. We were lucky to get out of this thing alive. It is *our* egg, and we should take it back to New York."

"It's staying in the valley of the Dune Dwellers, where it is being watched over by somebody with even more claim to it than we have. Get off the ownership crap, Granger. It won't wash with me and you know it."

"How dare you!"

"That egg, and whatever's inside it, belongs in that valley, period."

"I deserve credit for finding it, Jones."

"We all found the eggs, in a manner of speaking." Indy patted Loki's head, not wanting any more senseless argument. He gave the Mongols a final glance as he stood up. "Let's get out of here before they change their minds about feeding us to the dogs."

"This issue isn't settled," Granger said.

Indy gave his friend a steely look.

"No, I don't suppose it is at that," he said. "But we can settle it someplace else...some other time."

"Don't push me on this, Jones. I have every right to claim this discovery and you know it. For all the time I have known you, Jones, I have labored in obscurity while you sucked up the headlines. It's my turn for a little fame and fortune."

"Shut up," Indy told him. "We have some ponies to find."

Neither of them spoke on the long search for the ponies, or even after, during the longer ride back to the ravaged monastery in the Flaming Cliffs. With nowhere to keep the ponies while they entered the mountain, they again let them roam free.

They navigated the dangerous passageway in the dark with as much caution as they could muster, having gone without food or water for two blistering days and as many freezing nights. Indy led the way, walking a few yards in front of Granger across the sheer, narrow ledges. Loki trotted behind, his toenails clicking on the stone passageways.

Finally they emerged at the cavern that was the entrance to the lush valley as morning sunlight paled the skies beyond the towering sandstone peaks.

Indy paused a moment to take in this eerie primordial sight, allowing his eyes to wander across the traces of a Stone Age civilization below: the thatched huts and, farther down, the little shrine they had erected to the egg.

He wondered again if the wisdom of Urga's holy man might not have transcended all modern knowledge when he extracted a promise to protect the beast called *allergorhai-horhai*. Here, in the heart of Mongolia, awaited living answers to riddles having to do with the dawn of mankind and the end of the dinosaur age.

Indy felt his animosity toward Granger soften.

"It feels like home, doesn't it?" he asked.

"Yes," Granger allowed, "it does."

"Where is everybody?" Indy asked. "I don't see a sign of a living soul."

"That's because they're all down at the shrine," Granger said. "Look! I think the entire population is crowded down there. I think we may have arrived just in time, Jones."

Starbuck greeted them warmly outside the shrine.

He embraced Indy, but before he could do the same to Granger, the hunter put out his hand.

"Come and see what's happening!" Starbuck exclaimed as he pumped Granger's hand. "The egg is moving. Once in a while we can hear a tapping noise from inside the shell—I believe one of its developing horns is ready to break through. Quite possibly the smaller horn on the tip of its nose develops first to fulfill this purpose."

All of the People were crowded around the shrine, gesturing and talking excitedly in a language that neither Indy nor Granger pretended to understand. Then a young girl dropped to the ground and draped her arms around Loki, followed by several other of the children.

"Where's Joan?" Indy asked.

"She is with the egg, as always, my friend," Starbuck answered. "She sleeps with it and never leaves the shrine. There has been more movement the last two days. It may hatch at any moment."

"I guess they've never seen a dog," Indy said.

"Then we're even," Granger said. "I've never seen a triceratops."

"Where have you two been?" Starbuck asked. "We've been looking for you everywhere. You just seemed to disappear."

"We had some unfinished business to attend to," Indy said, but Starbuck was too excited to ask him to explain. The old man took Indy by the arm and led him through the Stone Age crowd to the center of the shrine.

Loki abandoned the children and followed his master, nosing his way through the tangle of legs and bare feet.

Joan was sitting beside the egg, a notebook in her lap. On the open page of the notebook was a sketch of the egg and the shrine.

"Miss me?" Indy asked.

"You don't know," she said, and looked away. "I didn't expect to see either of you again, alive or otherwise. My father didn't know where you had gone, but I did."

"That's why we didn't tell you," Indy said.

"I thought I would at least rate a good-bye."

"I was afraid you would talk me out of it," Indy said.

"Where's Tzi?" she asked.

"Dead," Indy answered. "Eaten by his own wild dogs. If it hadn't been for Loki, we never would have gotten out alive. He seems almost human. Any other dog couldn't have known what to do to help us."

"Some animals have rather remarkable intelligence." Starbuck reached down to scratch Loki's ear. He drew his hand back when Loki growled. "But then, others are poor judges of character."

Indy laughed.

Joan extended her hand. Loki smelled it, then accepted a few pets from her. "You poor fellow. You

look hungry and there are fresh wounds everywhere. But we'll fix you right up—"

A tapping sound interrupted her.

"There!" Starbuck said with great enthusiasm,
pointing to the egg with a trembling finger. "Listen
to it! The triceratops is almost ready to hatch. It
could come at any moment."

Granger pushed past Indy to approach the egg,
leaning over it as a soft, irregular tapping continued.
"It's alive," he said in a hushed voice. "The damn
thing's actually alive. When the world sees this we'll be
the most famous explorers on the face of the earth."

Indy pushed his fedora back on his head.

"Let's not count our dinosaurs before they're
hatched," he said pleasantly.

"We need to settle this," Granger said.

"You can't be serious about removing it," Starbuck
said. "I thought you agreed with me that there are too
many risks, taking it out from this valley across hundreds of miles of desert, then a voyage to America. A
thousand things could go wrong."

"He's right," Indy said. "Besides, how do you
plan getting it past the authorities at Urga? We
agreed that they could inspect whatever we took out
of the desert? Do you want to give *them* the greatest
find of the century?"

"We can smuggle it out," Granger said.

"Please," Starbuck pleaded. "You can't remove
it. There's an outside chance that another living egg

exists somewhere inside this valley—perhaps even another living triceratops. If you remove this egg, you will be dooming the species to certain extinction. And if you attempted to smuggle it out of Mongolia, you could end up killing it. What are you going to feed it? Do you know that the triceratops *eats* those wonderful late Cretaceous blooms that the People hung around your neck upon your arrival? Where are you going to find those on the outside?"

"Even if we had a dead specimen, it would be the most amazing thing the world has seen," Granger said. "I refuse to come back from this expedition empty-handed. Besides, Joan has been studying things here, and she will know how to take care of it on the way back."

"I'm not going back," Joan said.

"What?" Granger asked.

"I'm staying here," she said. "It's where I belong."

"What about your newspaper story?" Granger was incredulous. "Don't you ever want to see *that* in print?"

"It will be published, eventually." She smiled. "And I'm sure it will be a major story. But now is not the time. And the outside world is not for me."

"Utter nonsense," Granger argued. "You are just enamored of these good-looking bare-butted Stone Age lads. When you tire of them, you'll want to come back."

Joan shook her head.

"Have you all gone insane?" Granger shouted. "The three of you have no right to make a decision like this, keeping an earth-shattering zoological find from the outside world because you feel better qualified to study it in private. It's outrageous. This expedition was commissioned by the museum. Marcus Brody has a stake in this—he financed the whole thing as he has in the past, and what we found belongs to the museum. Brody has to be consulted and I'm quite sure what he'll have to say about it."

"Brody will agree," Indy said, "when I have a chance to explain things in private. And this will remain confidential, Granger, until Professor Starbuck here decides that the time is right."

Granger's eyes narrowed to slits.

"You're trying to cheat me out of the recognition I so richly deserve for leading you here, Jones," he railed. "I won't take it lying down."

He moved toward Indy with his hands doubling into fists.

"What is wrong with him?" Joan asked.

"I don't know," Indy said. "Maybe he's experiencing an aftereffect of that mushroom drink."

"So you think I'm insane, eh?"

"Take it easy, Granger," Indy protested. "Everyone will see to it that you're credited with guiding the expedition. All any of us wants is what is best for whatever is inside that egg. It will be safer here and you know it."

Granger halted a few inches from Indy's chest, his dark eyes flashing with smoldering anger.

"I won't let you take advantage of our friendship, Jones."

"I'm not—"

"I'm in charge of this expedition, if you'll remember, so back off and let me do my job. You have ruined everything you have touched on this journey. The dinosaur goes to New York and I won't let you stop me from taking it."

"Don't do this. You aren't thinking straight."

"There's nothing wrong with *my* thinking." Granger laughed. "But yours is out of line. Whatever is inside that egg is going back with me, and that's final."

"You aren't leaving me much choice." Indy sighed.

"Whew!" Joan said, attempting to change the subject. She put her arm around Indy's waist so that he wouldn't be able to lunge at Granger. "Is it me, or is it hot in here?"

"It's not the heat," Indy said. "It's the stupidity."

Granger swung a meaty fist toward Indy's jaw so quickly that Joan had no time to get out of the way.

Indy shoved Joan aside as he brought up a forearm to block Granger's heavy blow. Joan tumbled to the floor of the shrine just when Granger's fist landed on the muscle below his elbow. Indy felt sharp pain, wincing before he took a step back.

"You shouldn't have done that," he added in a voice like dry sand.

"To the devil with you, Jones!" Granger shouted, bringing his left fist whistling through the air in Indy's direction.

Cat-quick, Indy sidestepped the wild punch and swung a fist into Granger's belly, striking soft flesh that brought a grunt from deep in his throat. Granger's knees buckled momentarily, then he righted himself and reached for his stomach.

Indy threw a left jab, hitting bone above Granger's temple with enough force to crack knuckles, twisting his head violently to one side.

Granger staggered back near the shrine, blinking furiously to clear his addled brain.

"The egg!" Starbuck shouted, rushing toward Granger to block his path.

Granger shook his head, crouching down, his senses returned all at once. He leaped for Indy, looping a dangerous right hook at his opponent's cheek.

"Dammit, Granger!" Indy cried. "You're forcing me to knock some sense into your empty skull."

Granger's fist whispered past Indy's face, off by a mere few whiskers. This gave Indy an opening he hadn't counted on while his adversary was off balance. He drove a fist into Granger's belly again, not wanting to seriously hurt a friend who was, for the moment, out of control.

His punch brought a deeper groan from Granger, who fell back from the force of Indy's knuckles. He stumbled toward the shrine on rubbery legs, reeling back blindly, gasping for air.

"The egg!" Starbuck cried again.

Granger tripped, slamming against a much smaller and lighter Starbuck. Both men tumbled over the cradle that held the egg before they slumped to the dirt floor.

Joan screamed. In the same instant Indy was diving for the egg with arms outstretched. The precious egg teetered on an edge of the shrine, then it rolled off.

As if in slow motion the egg fell into Indy's hands, but the weight of it dropped his knuckles to the stone floor. A cracking sound echoed like thunder in the grotto, a sound that brought a groan of a different kind from Indy and Starbuck.

"It's broken!" Starbuck shrieked.

Joan wailed as though she was in pain.

In the dim light from the lamp, Indy saw the shell split in two places. Fluid leaked into his palms before the egg broke in half near its center. Bits of shell cascaded to the floor. Indy was left holding a sticky, squirming ball of rough skin and armor plate that was so heavy he moaned with effort.

A nightmarish face arose from the ball of flesh he tried to grip in his hands. Dark, reptilian eyes beheld him for a moment. A pair of knobs protruded above the eyes, two tiny horns in their earliest stage of formation. A single ivory-colored knob adorned the little creature's nose. Indy was struck immediately with how much it resembled a miniature rhinoceros.

Joan gasped. "It's a triceratops, and it's alive."

The creature made no sound. It stopped squirming in Indy's palms, moving its unsightly head toward the carbide light. Indy put it down gently on the grotto floor when Starbuck knelt beside it.

"A living fossil," Starbuck said with reverence. "It isn't a dream any longer."

The animal moved its short legs, testing them. In a moment of silence Granger groaned again, clasping both hands to his stomach.

A second later the triceratops planted its rear legs underneath its body and raised up unsteadily, hindquarters in the air. Next, it came to its front feet, swaying a little until it was sure of its balance.

And still it made no sound.

"I'll be damned," Indy whispered. "Here's the last dinosaur on earth and it's looking at us like we're the ones who don't belong here." Indy took his hands away, wiping the sticky fluid clinging to his palms and fingers on the straw.

Granger sat up, warning Indy to be ready for another round of flying fists.

"Look at this thing, Granger," Indy said, coming to his knees. "How can you or anyone else believe something so spectacular is worthy of being stuffed in a taxidermy shop? This creature is a part of something much larger than any of us can comprehend. We can't run the risk of doing anything that might upset nature's peculiar balance here. Some freakish twist of fate allowed this triceratops to escape extinction in this exact spot. It simply can't be removed. The odds against its survival are too high."

Granger struggled to his feet.

"Don't you think nature—or God, if you will—has some plan for this living, breathing anachronism? We can't kill it like we have killed other living things on the planet. I'm sure it would make one helluva hatband, Granger old boy, but it seems to me it's here for something more important."

Indy got up cautiously, keeping an eye on Granger's hands.

Granger studied the baby dinosaur for several thoughtful seconds. The animal simply stood there watching as four humans stared back at it.

"I'm sorry," Granger said, taking a deep breath. He wiped his mouth with the back of his hand. "I don't know what came over me. All I could think of was a lifetime of hardship with no reward."

"No reward?" Indy asked. "Granger, are you nuts?"

"Normally, no."

"Think of the adventures we've had together," Indy said. "How many other people can say they actually did something to make a difference in this world, instead of just going along with the crowd?"

"You can't put it in the bank," Granger complained.

"Friendship won't fit in a savings account either," Indy said, "but I wouldn't trade your friendship for all the money in the world. I know you hate those funny guys in the orange robes, but what they say about money makes sense."

"Sorry I lost my head just now," Granger said.

Starbuck distracted everyone by touching the dinosaur with the tip of a finger.

"He'll be getting hungry," Starbuck said. Then he spoke to one of the children outside the shrine. Soon, a willow basket full of colorful blossoms was brought to the shrine.

Starbuck offered the baby one of the flowers.

He sniffed at it and then took it in his parrotlike beak, munching happily.

"He's eating," Starbuck said excitedly.

A noise startled Indy and the others. It sounded like the grunt of a baby pig. The tiny triceratops blew through oblong nostrils at the end of a somewhat pudgy nose, its pointed lip curling toward Starbuck's finger.

"He said hello to us," Starbuck joked.

Joan knelt beside her father, staring at the baby with a look of utter fascination. "Welcome to the twentieth century," she said quietly. "You can't imagine how surprised we are to see you."

Indy turned back to Granger. Granger extended a handshake.

"I'm truly sorry for the way I behaved, Indy."

Indy rubbed sore knuckles, then grinned. "No need to say any more. All I want is your word on one thing . . . we never reveal the location of this valley to anyone, until Professor Starbuck and Joan agree that the time has come to show the world our secret."

"Agreed," Granger promised.

They shook hands.

Later, as Joan held the sleeping baby dinosaur in her arms, Indy sat down next to her.

"It's hard to imagine," she said. "This little ball of horn and skin will eventually grow to be over thirty feet long and weigh eight tons. A real monster."

"Why, Sister"—Indy grinned—"you seem almost *happy*."

"I am," she said. "For the first time in my life, I'm

thinking of something besides myself. My father needs me, and this little thunder lizard needs me as well. Two out of three ain't bad."

"What do you mean?" Indy asked.

"I had hoped you would round out this happy trinity."

Indy was silent.

She placed a hand on his arm. Then she leaned over, carefully so as not to disturb the sleeping baby, and kissed him with as much passion as she could muster in so awkward a position. Indy closed his eyes and could feel the world slip away.

"Stay with me," she urged.

"It's tempting," Indy said.

"Then why not?" she asked. "You'll never find another paradise like this one. No war, no crime, no need to worry about money. Everything you could hope for is here—and more."

"I agree," Indy said. "It *is* a paradise. And I think, in time, I could learn to forgive you for lying like a rug to me and Brody and Granger. Hell, who am I kidding? I already forgive you."

"Stay," she urged.

"I can't."

"Why not?"

"It's too easy," Indy said. "I want to forget all the hatred and disappointment that is in the world. But it would be just too damned *comfortable*. It feels wrong."

"What's so wrong about feeling good?" Joan asked.

"Nothing, if that's where your destiny leads you," he said. "But this isn't for me. My gut tells me I still have some things to do out there."

"And you're still in love with—"

"Alecia," Indy said.

Joan looked away.

"But I'm going back to the world knowing that you were the good person I thought you were when I first met you," Indy said. "Despite all that has happened on this journey, the cannibals and the privations, you have restored my faith in humanity. That is what I'm taking back with me. And the knowledge that you and your father are here, taking care of the past for the future."

"I'll miss you," she whispered.

"I'll miss you, too," Indy said. "But keep taking notes. Write that book. You owe it to the world. That's *your* destiny."

10

THE KNIFE OF GENGHIS KHAN

A desert wind blew hot and dry across Indy's sun-blistered skin. The crown of his hat was soaked with sweat and sand particles clung to his dampened neck and forearms. Loki trotted beside him, staying in his master's shadow to be out of direct sun.

Granger walked beside them, the Mauser slung like a pole across his shoulders.

Off to the south a range of tall mountains purpled in haze stirred up by the mighty steppe winds blasting across the open flats. A few stunted trees dotted the horizon here and there, offering scant shade for weary desert travelers. Indy knew that both he and Granger, and probably the dog, were too thirsty to go much farther. They had slung gourds filled with food and water over their shoulders before leaving the secret valley, but despite their best attempts at rationing, their supplies were now exhausted.

"Stop," Granger said.

"What is it?" Indy asked tiredly.

"Over there, Jones." Granger pointed. "On that ridge to the south. It's about four hundred yards, but I think I saw antelope."

Indy nodded.

"I'm going to attempt to bag it," Granger said. "It's worth a chance. We need meat, and we could drink the blood."

Indy made a face.

"You stay here," Granger said. "I can't get close enough for a shot with you and the dog in tow. Why don't you go take a rest in the shade of that rock over there. And stay put, because I need to be able to find you when I get back."

"No problem," Indy said. "I can use the rest."

Indy trudged over to the boulder and sat down with his back to the shady side. Loki followed and put his head on Indy's thigh, begging for affection.

"How're you doing?" Indy asked the dog. "Thirsty? So am I."

The dog panted happily.

They had waited in the shade of the rock for more than an hour when Loki growled.

"What is it, boy?"

The dog looked back at Indy with concerned

eyes, as if he understood. Then he growled again, hairs bristling along his back.

Indy was sure they were back in the territory controlled by Tzen Khan, so why did Loki sense trouble? Or had Granger's memory failed and led them into a region ruled by some other warlord?

Loki continued to growl.

The shepherd's good ear stood up, cocked in the direction of a sand dune a couple of hundred yards away. Indy trusted the dog's keen senses.

"Something's behind that dune," Indy said to himself. He stood, took the revolver from his belt, and moved cautiously forward.

When they had closed to within fifty feet of the top of the dune, Loki became hesitant. He whined softly, and looked at Indy with eyes that seemed to plead for them to go back.

"C'mon, Loki. Whatever's back there can't be all that bad. Tzi is dead, and that only leaves—"

Loki barked savagely when a distant figure rode over the top of the dune. A thick-chested Mongol atop a nervous chestnut stud halted his mount on the crest of the sand hill.

"That's General Tzi's stallion," Indy breathed. "Only he's dead. It looks like Tzi's lieutenant. At least he's ugly enough to be."

Indy knew Chang hadn't followed them just to be sociable.

It was a challenge, a fight Chang wanted. Indy

wondered why Chang would wait for another opportunity when he and the soldiers could have killed them at the ravine.

"I hope he came alone," Indy said.

Indy strode forward, deciding that any sign of cowardice would be fatal. Loki struck a trot to stay beside him, growling softly, ear pricked forward. The closer Indy came to the horse and rider, the surer he was of the Mongol's identity.

Chang had a carbine, and he rested the stock against one knee. He watched Indy approach without moving a muscle, holding his stud in check with a tight rein.

Indy was well within rifle range, and still Chang sat his horse like granite.

"What in the devil is he up to?" Indy asked Loki.

As they neared, Loki's growl became louder, a warning as plain as the dog could make it. Indy's boots crossed a slab of sandstone where footing was better, then on to the next stretch of sugary sand.

At the crest of the dune Indy stopped, watching Chang carefully, ready for any sudden move he might make to shoulder his rifle. Chang remained stock-still, while a gust of dry wind blew sand away from his horse's fidgeting hooves. Indy cast a hurried glance around him, making sure they were alone.

"Jones!" Chang shouted. "Where you hide big eggs?"

Loki snarled at the sound of Chang's voice.

"We don't have them."

"Tell me where is eggs or you die," Chang said, his face an unreadable stoic mask. "One monk tell general about eggs before he die. *Allergorhai-horhai* eggs."

"We got hungry," Indy said, "so we ate 'em."

Were soldiers hidden behind the dune? When Tzi died, surely Chang became the army's leader. Or was Chang in the prehistoric egg business by himself, so that profits didn't have to be divided among his relatives.

"Not funny," Chang said.

"Not kidding," Indy said.

A steady increase in westerly winds began to sweep bigger clouds of dust and sand across the plain. With a thick sand screen between them, Chang's aim might be off just enough to make him miss with a rifle.

"I kill unless you talk!"

"I am talking. The eggs broke. It was an accident, so we ate what was inside. It tasted terrible. Tough as rubber. Like bad chicken."

Now Chang's calm disappeared. He sent his horse forward in a walk, riding closer to Indy.

"Tell me, Jones, or I cut out your heart!"

Wind blasted across the dune, driving sand into the air in billowing swirls. Indy's hat almost blew off his head until he tilted its brim into the gust.

"Some people say I don't have a heart," Indy said. "There's a woman in England who said my heart was made of stone."

Chang urged the chestnut farther down the sandy slope, but as he approached he was quickly surrounded by gritty clouds of pale dust. Wind gusted, howling across the tops of surrounding sand dunes, screaming through apertures in rock formations, kicking up more dirt particles and sand as it swept across the land.

Now! Indy thought as the chestnut horse edged a little closer, fighting against the storm. Indy lunged and grabbed the barrel of Chang's carbine and pulled him from the saddle. Chang's foot caught in the stirrup.

The horse took off down the dune, dragging them both. Indy would not release his grip on the rifle for fear that Chang would make good on his promise to shoot him.

The chestnut struck an awkward gallop through deep sand drifts. Spits of windblown sand struck Indy's face and stung his eyes as he wrestled for the carbine. Chang pulled the trigger and the gun fired repeatedly. Although the barrel became hot, Indy would not let go.

Suddenly Chang's boot was free of the stirrup, and they were both tumbling down the side of a sand dune. Indy let go of the rifle, letting Chang spin away, while he grabbed his revolver and attempted a quick now-or-never shot.

Chang came to a stop and threw down on Indy.

The Webley's blast thundered above screeching winds, and Indy imagined he could hear the singsong flight of the bullet. Chang flew backward as the carbine cartwheeled from his hands.

The chestnut continued to run.

The cannibal lieutenant landed on his back, and slid on a moving carpet of sand to the base of the dune.

Loki barked his approval.

Sand peppered Indy's face until, as if by design, the wind died down enough to allow him to see Chang's body clearly.

"A lucky shot," Indy said to himself.

A dark red stain was widening on the Mongol's chest.

Indy walked down the dune cautiously, making sure Chang was not moving. When he was ten feet away he kept his revolver aimed in front of him.

Chang lay motionless, eyes closed, with blood streaming down his belly. Indy stood over him, casting a shadow across the spot where the Mongol had fallen. Blood seeped into the sand, disappearing when it trickled off Chang's ribs. His carbine lay a few feet away out of reach, a rusted Polish Karabin army rifle with its stock scarred by long use and neglect.

When Indy was satisfied that Chang was unconscious, he squatted down to check the body for any sign of a pulse. He reached for Chang's throat to touch a carotid artery.

Chang's eyes flew open—he made a grab for Indy's shirtfront and seized a fistful of fabric while his other hand formed a claw to scratch across Indy's face.

Fingernails tore into Indy's cheeks.

Indy leaped backward, wielding his gun like a club to strike Chang's jaw. The barrel of his Webley slammed into skin and bone with a dull thump, yet Indy was blinded by the Mongol's palm and he had only the sound and feel of his blow by which to judge the force of its impact. He heard a grunt as he fell back on his rump. At the same time Chang's fingers relaxed their ironlike grip on his cheeks and forehead.

Chang tumbled over on his side kicking, making a sound like a wounded animal. A tiny fountain of red squirted by his right ear where a plug of skin dangled from his scalp. The front sight on Indy's .38 was bloody—a sliver of flesh dangled from it until he wiped it off on his pant leg.

Indy scrambled to his feet breathing heavily and his heart was pounding like a drum. "That was close," he wheezed, after taking stock of his condition. When he touched his face a trace of red smeared his fingers.

Chang cupped a brown palm over the hole above his ear. He fell silent and rolled over on his back. The look he gave Indy was one of pure hatred.

"The hot breath of Buddha save you, Jones," he gasped with a great deal of effort, pink foam bubbling from his lips, indicating a torn lung where Indy's bullet had pierced his chest. "The Brilliant One spare your life by making wind blow...." He coughed up a mouthful of blood.

"You had your chance to leave it alone, Chang."

"You have egg of *horhai*. It belong to us."

Indy pounded his fist in the sand.

"Why do all of you tough guys insist on *ownership*?" he asked. Chang was dying and for some strange reason he wanted to explain. "The egg hatched. The *horhai* lives."

Chang blinked.

"*Horhai* lives?" he asked, spitting blood down his chin when he spoke.

Indy nodded. "It lives," he said. "If nothing goes wrong—and if nobody bothers them, the *horhai* may come back as a species. My friends are scientists and they know what they're doing."

Chang's eyes began to cloud with death.

"Enlightened One must want it to be," he said. Then he lifted his hand and regarded the blood on his fingers and palm. "And this." Chang smiled.

"Next time," he said, "I not follow False Lama."

His eyelids fluttered closed, he coughed a final

time, and he stopped breathing. After a moment there was a rush of air from his mouth as his lungs emptied.

"I hope not," Indy whispered.

He got up and brushed the sand from his palms.

Then he hesitated. He looked at the body, then at Loki, who was sniffing Chang's pant leg.

"C'mon, boy," Indy said. "We're not that hungry."

Loki hesitated a moment, sniffed the wind, then followed Indy away from the dune. Even before they had returned to the boulder, the wind began to scour away their footprints and other signs of the desperate struggle.

Loki put his nose in the air and began to bark.

Cranking over the dunes was the most curious contraption Indy had ever seen. It was the expedition's third truck, the one that had been left behind at Kalgan, only it was being pulled by a team of horses.

The windshield had been knocked out and Wu Han sat in the driver's seat, but instead of a steering wheel, he had a pair of reins in his hands. The back of the truck was piled high with supplies.

Granger sat in the passenger seat, laughing. On the hood of the truck was an antelope.

"Dr. Jones!" Wu Han called through the vacant

windshield. "At last I have found you, after searching the length and breadth of the Gobi. I told you to
count on me!"

"Wu Han," Indy breathed. "What have you done
to our truck?"

"I'm sorry, but this is what the blacksmith had in
mind when he said he could fix it," Wu Han said. "I
hope you aren't angry. It is slow, but reliable."

"I'm not angry, Wu Han," Indy said. "I'm just
glad to see you. And you're right—you did come
through when we needed you. Now we can ride
back in comfort, even if our truck only has two
horsepower instead of a hundred."

Granger handed Indy a canteen.

Indy poured some water out in the palm of his
hand and let Loki lap it up. Then he took a long
drink himself.

"Where's Sister Joan?" Wu Han asked.

"Heaven," Indy said.

"I'm sorry," Wu Han replied, his head bowed.

"Don't be," Indy said. "She's with her father,
which is what she wanted all along."

"Yes," Wu Han said. "I can understand that."

Indy took the expedition flag from his pocket.
Wu Han found a long pole, and together they
mounted it over the cab of the truck.

It unfurled and snapped in the wind.

"There," Indy said. "What do you think?"

"Well," Granger remarked as he leaned against

the truck, "it's not what I had in mind, but it will do. A fitting end to the most backward expedition I've ever seen. Instead of bringing things out of the Gobi, we saw how much we could leave *here*."

An oasis beckoned at the bottom of a shallow valley, emerald green against brown sandstone on an arid plain. A Mongol warrior on a dappled gray pony approached Indy from a rock formation overlooking Khan's village of yurts, a lookout posted nearby to prevent a surprise attack.

Indy halted the team, awaiting permission to drive down to speak with Khan. The sentry galloped up and reined down hard in a cloud of dust. The Mongol was short, wiry, with a long scar down his cheek and traces of pockmarks on his skin, a survivor of the smallpox outbreak. Indy thought he remembered seeing this man with Khan.

"You are Dr. Jones," he said in halting English. He carried a very old Mosin Russian rifle, which he lowered in surprise as soon as he saw Loki. The dog was trotting beside the truck.

"We are here to pay our respects to the Great Khan," Indy said. "I have news of the death of General Tzi and the destruction of the False Lama."

"We have heard," the sentry said. "The exalted Tzen Khan is in the desert asking Buddha to show him nirvana, where there is no pain, no sorrow, no desire. He seeks a vision. He still grieves for his family."

Again the sentry's gaze fell on Loki.

"This is your dog?"

"Yes, of course," Indy said. "He is the one who saved us from General Tzi and his band of dogs and cannibals."

"Wonderful!" the sentry said.

"I'm glad you're pleased," Indy said, somewhat confused.

The Mongol grinned. "Khan will be very grateful for this wonderful news. More than anything, for the safe and unexpected return of his friend."

"I'm glad to be here," Indy said. "Tell me where I can find him."

"In the desert to the north. There is a holy mountain where Khan goes to pray. You can see it in the distance if you look closely with your heart."

He pointed.

Indy saw the faint outline of a bald mountain on the horizon despite the blowing sand clouds, which had become their ever-present companion.

"Come with me," the sentry said, wheeling his gray. "I am called Turi, and if you wish I will take you to our camp, then give you a horse so you can visit Khan at the sacred place."

Indy flicked the reins and the horse-drawn truck followed, with Loki running behind.

"Do you Mongols go everywhere at a full gallop?" Indy shouted, holding on to his hat.

"Life is short!" Turi shouted. "The desert is vast. You go slow, you see little. You go fast, you see much!"

"Where did you learn to speak such good English?"

"American missionaries came to Urga when I was a boy, before the Communists drove them out," Turi said. "The father of Tzen Khan sent us both there for learning."

They drove down to a spring pool surrounded by rocks and a few stunted trees. Dozens of tents had been erected around the pool. Curious villagers came out to watch them ride in. Some pointed to Loki and began talking excitedly among themselves.

Turi shouted to a tribesman. Moments later a group of women hurried from one of the tents carrying clay vessels of water and bowls of smoked goat meat. Indy was offered a jar of dark red wine, which he politely declined while a young Mongol boy came to the pool leading a bridled bay gelding bearing a typical Mongolian wood saddle.

Indy ate goat meat while Loki ate his fill as well.

"Take care of the team," he told Wu Han. "Granger, are you coming with me?"

"No, Jones, I think not," Granger said. "You and Khan seem to have some sort of spiritual bond which I don't pretend to understand. I will just stay here and grow fat on goat's milk."

"Suit yourself," Indy said, taking the reins on his borrowed bay. "Can we leave, Turi? I'd like to get there before sundown."

"I understand, Dr. Jones," Turi said. "You wish to make Khan happy so that his long quest for inner peace may end."

Turi swung up on his dappled pony, then shouted something in his native dialect to villagers standing near the pool.

A cheer went up all around the village.

"What did you tell them?" Indy asked.

"I told them that you and Loki are responsible for the death of Tzi and the False One. Perhaps now there will be less fighting between us."

Indy mounted and looked down at Loki.

"Coming?" he asked. "I know your paws are sore and this would be a good place for a rest. You can stay if you'd like."

"Jones, you've gone insane," Granger shouted. "You think that dog can understand you?"

Loki barked.

Indy couldn't help but grin.

"This one does," he replied.

The mountain loomed above the desert floor, a craggy mass of huge sandstone slabs tilted oddly, as though the earth beneath it was slightly out of kilter when volcanic forces pushed it through to the surface. Indy looked over his shoulder to watch dust from Turi's horse boil into a cloudless evening sky as he rode back to his village.

Near sunset the fierce desert winds died, leaving empty land around the mountain as still as quiet water. Indy rode slowly to the base of a steep slope, where he got down, leaving his pony to graze on short, sun-curled grass between piles of rock.

It was then that he noticed Loki's strange behavior. The Alsatian looked up at the mountain and began to whimper. It was a sound almost akin to human crying, unlike any noise the dog had ever made before.

"You know who's up there?" Indy asked.

Loki turned his pale blue eyes on Indy, and the moment Indy saw them he knew instinctively that they did not belong to an animal. "The question is," Indy whispered, "who are *you*?"

Loki stared at him a moment longer, then he started up the mountain alone. Indy stood there until he realized he was being left behind, and he began to scramble up the rocks.

Half an hour was needed to approach the peak. Loki limped badly near the top, winding his way between boulders, appearing again on barren slabs of stone with Indy close on his heels. A silence gripped the mountaintop, only the sounds of Indy's boots interrupting the quiet. Almost out of breath, Indy gave the last few yards every ounce of determination he possessed, until he came out on a flat spot overlooking miles of desert in every direction.

On the far side of the plateau a figure in a flowing robe stood with his face to the sky, palms outstretched. Even when he was imploring the All-Powerful for mercy, Khan cut a figure of nobility.

Indy hurried toward him, but it was Loki who found new energy, breaking into a run across the plateau until he reached Khan's side.

Khan turned suddenly, startled. He saw Indy, then he looked down at the animal near his feet. He slowly lowered his hands to his sides.

Indy walked over, reading Khan's expression as he stumbled to a halt. "I don't believe you expected to see us again," he said quietly, out of breath after the difficult climb.

Khan shook his head as he knelt down.

"No," he said in a distant voice, reaching for Loki's nose.

Loki licked Khan's hand gently, but he made no sound.

"Buddha's first great truth is that life is suffering," Khan said. "I had climbed this mountain seeking understanding of that truth, to shoulder my great sorrow. And now I find that the universe is laughing with joy."

"What do you mean by that?" Indy asked.

"You have returned my best friend to me."

"What?"

"The dog," Khan said. "He has always been my best friend, during several lives. The Buddha reincarnated him as a dog for this one."

"But—"

"Tzi cut off his ear and sent it to me," Khan said. "I feared that he was dead. But I see now that Tzi attempted to make him a part of the dog pack, to force him to eat human flesh or starve."

"It didn't work," Indy said.

"Of course not," Khan said. "A spirit as great as Zolo's cannot be broken by torture."

"This is hard to believe," Indy said. "I was sort of hoping to keep the dog for my own."

Khan laughed.

"You would be better hoping to own the wind."

"So this dog is the reincarnation of your old buddy—what's his name, Zolo?—that has been at your side for several thousand years, that's what you're trying to tell me?"

"I can only tell you this, Marco Polo/Indiana Jones. There are things in this world we do not always understand. As mortals, we can only know what a mortal can know."

Khan fixed his gaze on Indy.

"This is not a dog, nor can I explain what he is. It is written that only a Lama can see true enlightenment. Buddha reveals all knowledge of what lies beyond only to those who take his vows. This will be very hard for you to believe; however, I can only tell you that this animal is much more than what he seems. He is the embodiment of an ally and friend, long-dead and yet unborn, a place of habitation for a man's soul."

Indy hesitated a moment.

"I believe," he said sadly, "that there is something special about this dog. If you say that he is your friend, then I am glad that you are reunited."

Khan smiled.

"You are very wise for one who does not know the path to enlightenment."

Khan touched the top of Loki's head affectionately and said something in a foreign tongue Indy did not understand. Loki rested on his haunches, watching Khan's face intently.

"He saved my life," Indy said. "He killed Tzi."

Khan's smile widened.

"He has avenged the death of my family well," Khan said. "Of course, the False One is dead as well if this is so."

"Yes," Indy said.

"Splendid. I hope he suffered."

"Khan," Indy said. "I am somewhat attached to this dog. I will miss him, but this is where he belongs, and I guess I've known that all along."

Khan came to his feet and embraced Indy.

"You are indeed a good friend. You have saved many of my people from smallpox, and now you return with my closest companion. I must find a way to repay you for all of your kindness."

"You owe me nothing," Indy said.

"Nonsense," Khan said.

"What we found in the desert was payment enough."

"You found what you were looking for?"

"And more," Indy said.

He turned to the sunset.

"I should be going," Indy said. "My friend in New York anxiously awaits word. Unfortunately, we do not have the excellent system of water-hole telegraph."

He reached down and gave Loki a scratch behind his ear.

"So long, partner. We had our share of close calls. Thanks for warning me about Chang, and thanks for what you did when Tzi found us."

The shepherd panted in response.

"Wait," Khan said.

He opened his robe and drew out a dagger with a strangely curved blade. The handle sparkled with brilliant jewels, rubies and emeralds and sapphires.

"This is the knife of Genghis Khan," he said. "It has been handed down in my family for many generations. Let this be a symbol of our friendship for as long as we both shall live—and beyond!"

Khan extended the knife in both hands.

"I can't accept it," Indy protested. "It must be worth a fortune."

"Bah!" Khan said. "True worth is measured in the hearts of one's friends. Take it!"

Indy allowed Khan to place the knife handle in his palm. It was then he saw etchings on the blade, a map of sorts and an inscription, difficult to read in fading sunlight.

"What are these markings?" Indy asked.

"A secret," Khan said, "that even I cannot decipher. This knife was said to be old even in the Great Khan's time."

His face turned grave.

"Can you read it, Indiana Jones?"

"Perhaps with some work," Indy said. "These characters appear to be the name of Qin-Shi-Huang, the first emperor of China. I know very little—nobody does, really—other than that his tomb is reputed to be a scale model of the universe, with jewels portraying the constellations and constantly flowing streams of mercury representing the rivers."

"Now you play upon my disbelief," Khan said.

"Well, that's the story," Indy said. "I didn't say it was true. Thank you for such a beautiful gift. It will remain one of my prized possessions."

Indy tucked the knife in his belt.

"Farewell," Khan said. "May your journey be safe—but not too safe. That would be boring!"

Indy smiled. "I could stand to be bored for a while."

"Then, may you find peace." Khan gazed across

the desert as purple shadows formed below rocks and sand dunes. "Inner peace comes from the mind," he said knowingly. "It has no special place, no special time. Buddha has granted all men the opportunity to find peace. So few know where to look for nirvana. It lives within the minds of men."

Indy stuck out his hand. "See you next time around," he said.

"Good-bye, Indiana Jones," Khan said. "And be careful of what you go in search of—you just might find it."

They shook, and Indy gave Loki one last pat on the head. Then he left and did not look back.

Three weeks later the horse-drawn truck rolled into Kalgan. They sold the contraption to the blacksmith, then used the money to buy passage on the train to Shanghai. While they waited to board the train, Indy prepared a cable for Brody. It read:

MARCUS BRODY
C/O AMERICAN MUSEUM OF NATURAL
HISTORY

NEW YORK CITY
FOUND STARBUCK STOP LOST PARADISE
STOP WIRE MONEY TO CATHAY HOTEL
SHANGHAI STOP JONES STOP END

They boarded the train at Kalgan, leaving the Shen Shei peaks behind. The pounding of the steam locomotive seemed to ease Indy back toward the twentieth century.

"Well, Jones," Granger said. "Do you suppose the world will ever know? Or will Starbuck and his daughter simply become lost in the mists of time?"

"I can't say that I would blame them," Indy said, looking out the window at a truck convoy of Chinese troops with bristling bayonets, waiting for the train to pass. "And I wonder if we aren't the ones lost in time, hurtling forward with all the sound and fury of a dive-bomber."

Epilogue

GRAVE OF THE U-357

Off the coast of Denmark
December 31, 1933

The *U-357* had torn open her starboard ballast tanks while attempting to put into a narrow fjord where an unmarked truck waited to take the Crystal Skull to Berlin.

Driven by the fear of ripping open her pressure hull on the jagged rocks, the captain of the *U-357* had limped her back out to sea, but had discovered too late the true extent of the damage to the ballast tanks. The air trapped in the recesses of her starboard tank provided enough buoyancy to maintain the boat in the shallow fjord, but as more water and pressure built above her decks in the open sea, the critical balance between floating and sinking had been lost in a fraction of a second. Despite the best efforts of her electric motors to drive the boat back to the surface, the *U-357* had yielded to the inevitable embrace of the deep.

She had gone down bow-first in a hundred and twenty feet of water and, without the use of the starboard tank, had been unable to regain positive buoyancy. There had not been time to trail a long wire, the underwater antenna needed to communicate at depth, so the location of her final resting place remained a mystery to Berlin. Even the jackbooted men who waited in the truck were unsure of her location, since she had entered the fjord submerged and under radio silence. The time and coordinates of the transfer had been established days before.

Her crew had no choice but to brace themselves for a white-knuckled ride of no return as the submarine slid deeper and deeper into the freezing waters. When her bow finally snubbed against the bottom, flooding the forward torpedo room but leaving the rest of the hull uncompromised, a spontaneous cheer had erupted from the crew. It was not for any hope of rescue—each and every man knew the boat was beyond hope—but from a sense of relief. They would eventually suffocate, choking on the poison expelled from their own lungs, instead of drowning. They spent the time waiting playing cards, reading, or writing a last letter to families that would never read it.

Indiana Jones found the submarine at the coordinates Belloq had provided, although he had not expected the boat to be perched on a shelf overlooking a five-hundred-foot drop. Belloq had not volunteered to Indy how he knew the location of the missing submarine when Berlin did not, or why he had chosen to share this information. The latter, Indy suspected, had to do with the Nazi's treatment of Belloq—*Bellosh!*—as an employee. But whatever his reason, Indy didn't care. The important thing was that the Crystal Skull was again tantalizingly within his reach, if not quite within his grasp.

But soon, Indy told himself as the brass diving helmet was bolted into place over the breastplate of the nylon diving suit. Soon. Then he stepped off with his lead boots into the freezing waters and began his descent.

He landed almost on the deck of the *U-357*, thanks to good soundings by the crew of the French salvage ship *Jules Verne*. Although he had done some hard-hat diving before, he had never attempted such a deep or a cold dive. His breath was coming in gasps. He forced himself to gain control before proceeding.

Walking across the bottom of the ocean in comical, exaggerated steps, Indy made his way to the bow of the submarine and entered the torpedo room through the gap in her hull. He was careful not to snag his air lines on the jagged edges, and he pulled plenty of slack in with him in order to be able to move freely inside.

He snapped on the diving lamp at his belt.

He took a wrench from his belt and laboriously turned the mechanism in the center of the pressure door between the torpedo room and the rest of the boat. Air bubbles—the last air the crew had breathed—streamed from the perimeter of the door as the interior equalized to ambient water pressure. He could also feel a groan shake the boat from stem to stern as her weight shifted.

The door opened freely on its hinges.

Indy stepped awkwardly through the bulkhead and proceeded down the hall. There was plenty of paper and trash floating in the clear, cold water, but no sign of a yellow canister. Indy proceeded to the officers' quarters, a few yards down the hall, and opened the cabin door.

Kroeger floated out of the cabin like a ghost, his arms extended toward Indy, his blond hair washing back and forth over his perfect forehead.

Indy jumped, hitting the back of his head against the diving helmet. Instinctively he put his gloved hand up to the helmet in an attempt to rub the sore spot, but of course he couldn't.

Indy pulled Kroeger's body out of the doorway, then took the diving lamp from inside his belt and shone it over the interior of the cabin. Time was running short. The crew of the *Jules Verne* had said that at this depth, Indy would have only about fifteen minutes to search the wreck. If he ignored that time limit, he would risk the bends. Indy was about to leave the officers' quarters when a thought occurred to him.

He shone the light upward.

The yellow canister floated against the ceiling.

Indy tugged the canister down and placed it beneath his arm, then began to trudge back down the corridor the way he had come. Even though his arms and legs were freezing, inside the diving helmet sweat rolled from Indy's forehead and dripped into his eyes.

He had almost made it to the torpedo-room bulkhead when he felt the deck shift beneath his feet. Suddenly the hallway had tipped over on its side as the *U-357* rolled to port and inched a little farther over the shelf.

It was difficult to walk against the curved interior of the pressure hull. Indy stumbled over the pipes and other equipment that were secured to the wall. So he tried swimming. That didn't work, because of the lead boots. He could kick, but he didn't get anywhere. Finally, he grasped his air line and began to haul himself along toward the bow with his right hand. His left arm was fighting the buoyant yellow canister.

As he squeezed through the bulkhead door the boat shuddered and began to fall backward over the cliff. Indy lost his hold on the canister, which became entangled in the mass of pipes and fittings in the torpedo room.

Desperately, he pulled himself through the torpedo room and out of the gash in the hull. The bow of the *U-357* scooted along the bottom toward the abyss, threatening to suction Indy down with it. Indy jerked frantically on the lifeline to signal the crew to haul him up.

On the deck of the *Jules Verne,* the crew removed Indy's helmet. Behind him, the pump used to force air down the line spun to a stop.

"What happened?" the dive master asked, a cigarette dangling from the corner of his mouth.

"I had it," Indy said. "I had it under my arm and then the submarine shifted and started to go over the edge. I had to let go of it and get out."

"That is the way with wrecks," the dive master said. "Opening, closing hatches, shifting weight, you never know what will happen. But at least you made it out alive, monsieur."

Indy looked up as the other members of the crew rushed to the side and pointed. When the *U-357* reached the end of her long plunge to the seafloor beneath the shelf, her hull had buckled and broken in two, freeing all manner of buoyant debris: hats, clothing, unused life vests, tins of food.

"Look!" Indy shouted.

A yellow canister had popped to the surface and was bobbing happily among the waves.

"Bring us around," Indy said. "Let's haul it in."

As the *Jules Verne* came about, however, another yellow canister emerged, two hundred yards away. Suddenly there was a third and a fourth, and finally a score of yellow canisters that covered several acres of water.

The crew hauled one after another aboard only to discover they were oil drums, but resembled the type of gas canister in which Belloq had packed the skull.

"I'm sorry," the captain told Indy. "We cannot catch them all. Wind, tide, currents..."

Afterword

Indiana Jones and the Dinosaur Eggs was inspired by the expeditions of Roy Chapman Andrews to Outer Mongolia in the 1920s. These expeditions, which made headlines around the world for the discovery of the first dinosaur eggs (fossilized, alas!) known to science, were sponsored by the American Museum of Natural History in New York.

The discovery fired the imagination of the world because, at that time, scientists still did not know how dinosaurs bore their young. The adventure was also downright romantic, because Outer Mongolia was one of the few places left on earth that could legitimately be called *terra incognita*.

A few words about Andrews, the museum that he

made famous (or perhaps it was the other way around), and other matters related to this original Indiana Jones adventure, are in order.

Roy Chapman Andrews

Andrews is often cited as the inspiration—along with Saturday-afternoon adventure serials and the James Bond movies—for the character known as Indiana Jones. Whether Indy co-creators George Lucas and Steven Spielberg had Andrews in mind or not, he was in many ways a real-life Indiana Jones: smart, brave, resourceful, and often at the center of discovery and controversy.

A black-and-white photograph of Andrews in *The New Conquest of Central Asia,* a massive book about his fossil-hunting adventures in Mongolia, shows him posing with a cluster of dinosaur eggs. He is dressed in khaki, from his belt hangs a holstered revolver, and his eyes are shaded by a wide-brimmed hat. If you mentally add the bullwhip, you have a scene that could have been plucked from any of the Indiana Jones films.

Andrews was born on January 26, 1884, in Beloit, Wisconsin, during a thirty-below-zero winter storm. After graduating from college, he set out for New York—he had earned traveling money by doing taxidermy—bent on fulfilling his childhood ambition of working for the American Museum of Natural History. When he presented himself and the museum director explained that there were absolutely no jobs available, Andrews offered to scrub floors. When asked how a young man with a college education could be serious about such a menial position, Andrews said that it wasn't just any floors they were talking about—it was the *museum's* floors.

After a few months of wielding a mop and helping out with odd jobs, Andrews got his first real break by being assigned to help in the construction of a life-size model of a blue whale. The whale, which was to hang in the third-floor gallery, had turned into a major disappointment for the museum because its paper covering sagged, making it look hungry rather than majestic. Andrews solved the problem by coming up with a wire-mesh-and-papier-mâché skin for the whale.

From there, it was on to increasingly more challenging tasks as Andrews was sent around the world to collect real whales for the museum. Eventually he was asked by a publisher to write an article about whales and whaling, which led to another lifelong passion for Andrews: writing about his adventures.

After a stint in China that involved some shadowy connection with army intelligence during the First World War, Andrews returned to the museum and in 1920 proposed to director Henry Fairfield Osborn a plan so ambitious that it bordered on the foolhardy: an expedition into the little-known Gobi Desert that would attempt to reconstruct the entire past history of the Central Asian plateau. This meshed perfectly with Osborn's conviction that the area was the prehistoric staging ground for the world's human and animal life. Mongolia, Osborn believed, would be that place where humanity's much-touted evolutionary "missing link" would be found.

In April 1922, Andrews led the first expedition into Mongolia, a place that had not been previously noted for fossils. In fact, only a single rhinoceros tooth had ever been found. But four days after crossing the Great Wall into Outer Mongolia, the expedition found a cornucopia of fossils literally at their feet. In 1923, the expedition discovered fossilized dinosaur eggs in the area they had christened the Flaming Cliffs.

The expeditions that continued during the 1920s resulted in the museum's acquisition of an encyclopedic collection of fossils and established Mongolia as one of the richest fossil beds in the world. But because of changes in the area's political climate since the Red Russians had won control of it, the last expedition occurred in 1930.

Although none of the expeditions found anything that even remotely resembled a missing link, Andrews remained convinced to his dying day that the evolutionary Garden of Eden lay buried in Mongolia, just waiting to be discovered.

Although Andrews had many other adventures, and continued to write books about them, nothing was to rival the glory of the 1923 field season on the Mongolian plateau.

In 1933, Andrews took Osborn's place as director of the museum. The museum was at a low point. It had been hit hard by the Depression, and all field-work had been curtailed. Unfortunately, this time Andrews was unequal to the task at hand, but because of his fame, he lingered for years in the director's chair. Finally, in 1941, on the advice of a troubleshooter that had been brought in to evaluate the museum, the board of trustees asked Andrews to resign.

Andrews retired to Carmel, California, where he died in 1960.

Although most of Andrews's books are out of print, he was a popular writer in his day and many can still be found in the collection of any metropolitan public library. Titles to look for include his autobiography, *Under a Lucky Star* (1943), and a collection of true stories called *Heart of Asia* (1951). Some of his natural-history works are *Whale Hunting with Gun and Camera* (1916), *The New Conquest of Central Asia* (1932), and *This Amazing Planet* (1941).

The American Museum of Natural History
In the early years of the twentieth century a mop-wielding employee by the name of Roy Chapman Andrews called the museum "the most wonderful place in New York," and many would agree with that assessment today.

Located at Eighty-first Street and Central Park West, the museum is a labyrinth of interlocking buildings containing thousands of exhibits that invite weeks of careful exploration. The complex also includes the Naturemax Theatre and the Hayden Planetarium.

Among the museum's most popular exhibits are a ninety-foot fiberglass model of a blue whale (it has replaced the papier-mâché model that hung for decades); the largest meteorite ever found in the United States; and many thousands of dinosaur fossils, including several dozen eggs. Visitors should be careful, however, if the fossils bring the name of Roy Chapman Andrews to their lips—unofficial museum shorthand for rough treatment of a specimen is to "RCA" it, from Andrews's reputation for getting things done in the most direct way possible.

The museum was founded in 1869 by Albert S. Bickmore, a naturalist who had a vision of establishing the nation's leading natural-history museum in the nation's foremost city. Over the years the museum has become a city unto itself, including the publication of its own nationwide magazine, *Natural History*. But in addition to its role as an irreplaceable scientific resource, the museum's pursuit of understanding the natural world has also become an important spiritual resource for many Americans.

The memorial service for Joseph Campbell, the mythologist who with Bill Moyers mesmerized public-television audiences in the 1980s with *The Power of Myth*, was held at the American Museum of Natural History. As a boy, Campbell had stared in awe at the museum's exhibits of Native American masks and totems. That awe inspired him to a lifetime of spiritual adventure.

Although many articles and several books have been published about the museum over the years, one of the best is a volume by Douglas J. Preston called *Dinosaurs in the Attic* (1986). The book contains a wealth of anecdotal material about the museum's collections.

The Allergorhai-Horhai

Although somewhat different-looking from its counterpart in *Indiana Jones and the Dinosaur Eggs*, the *allergorhai-horhai* is the legendary sandworm of the Gobi Desert. Andrews wrote that all northern Mongols believed in it, but that he had never run across anyone claiming to have actually seen one.

"It is said to be about two feet long," Andrews said, "the body shaped like a sausage, and to have no head or legs; it is so poisonous that even to touch it means instant death."

Andrews concluded that although the beast was *probably* mythical, there might be some shred of truth in the legend because all of the descriptions he had heard of it were so similar.

The Sixty-Million-Year-Old Fish

Science sometimes stumbles across an animal that it previously declared extinct, and that's what happened in 1938 when a South African fishing trawler brought up in its nets a curious-looking fish called the *coelacanth*.

It was the first live specimen of the fish that had ever been found, and the next youngest (and obviously dead) specimen that science had was sixty million years old. Older specimens went back more than four hundred million years, older even than the oldest dinosaurs.

Since the advent of diving submersibles, many live coelacanths have been observed on the ocean floor, at depths of around six hundred feet—but only in the Indian Ocean, where that first one was hauled aboard. In 1965, however, a hundred-year-old silver religious artifact was discovered in Spain that appeared to be a detailed representation of the distinctive-looking coelacanth. The discovery asked the following question: How did a nineteenth-century Spaniard know what the fish looked like?

ABOUT THE AUTHOR

MAX McCOY is an award-winning journalist and author whose Bantam novels include *The Sixth Rider* and *Sons of Fire*. He lives in Pittsburg, Kansas.